He began to press hot kisses to Josie's throat before claiming her mouth.

Their desire swept her along like a swollen current of the river, like gale force winds that bent the tops of trees. She felt wild, free…cherished. She—

'No!'

Kent jerked back and glared. Through the haze of her desire she saw the torment in his eyes. His fingers bit into her shoulders and he shook her, but she had a feeling it was himself he wanted to shake. She made a move to reach out to him, to try and wipe away the pain that raked his face, but he dropped his hands and stepped back out of her reach.

'This is not going to happen,' he ground out.

Her arms felt bereft, cold. She gulped. Need lapped at her. What had she done wrong?

Dear Reader

I am thrilled to be writing for Mills & Boon in their centenary year. For one hundred years Mills & Boon have provided uplifting, emotionally satisfying, life-affirming stories. Stories that reflect the changing attitudes of the times, stories reflecting the feistiness and courage of our favourite heroines...and the heart-melting sexiness of our favourite heroes.

I have always loved reading romances—stories that leave a smile on my face. Now I love writing romances I can share with others. Creating heroines I can relate to, heroes I can drool over...and giving them the happy-ever-after they deserve in a world where happy-ever-afters aren't always guaranteed. I'm honoured my stories have found a home with such a wonderful publisher.

Happy centenary, Mills & Boon, may you flourish for the next hundred years.

Warm wishes

Michelle

Michelle would love readers to visit her at her website,
www.michelle-douglas.com

THE LONER'S
GUARDED HEART

BY
MICHELLE DOUGLAS

MILLS & BOON®

Pure reading pleasure

First published in Great Britain 2008
Harlequin Mills & Boon Limited,
Eton House, 18-24 Paradise Road, Richmond, Surrey TW9 1SR

© Michelle Douglas 2008

ISBN: 978 0 263 20249 6

Set in Times Roman 10½ on 12¾ pt
07-0208-48524

Printed and bound in Great Britain
by Antony Rowe Ltd, Chippenham, Wiltshire

Just like having a heart-to-heart
with your best friend, these stories will
take you from laughter to tears and back again!

Curl up and have a

HEART TO HEART

with
Mills & Boon® Romance

So heartwarming and emotional
you'll want to have some tissues handy!

**Look out for the next Heart to Heart
THE ITALIAN'S CINDERELLA BRIDE
by Lucy Gordon
in June**

For Greg

CHAPTER ONE

'HELLO?'

Josie Peterson bent down and called her greeting into the half-open window before knocking on the door again.

No movement. No sound. Nothing.

Chewing her lip, she stepped back and surveyed the front of the cottage—weatherboard, neatly painted white. A serviceable grey-checked gingham curtain hung at the windows.

Grey? A sigh rose up through her. She was tired of grey. She wanted frills. And colour. She wanted fun and fanciful.

She could feel the grey try to settle over her shoulders.

She shook herself and swung away, took in the view about her. The paths were swept, the lawns were cared for, but there wasn't a single garden bed to soften the uniformity. Not even a pot plant. At the moment, Josie would kill for the sight of a single cheerful gerbera, let alone a whole row of them.

Six wooden cabins marched down the slope away from the cottage. Nothing moved. No signs of habitation greeted her. No cars, no towels drying on verandas, no pushbikes or cricket bats leant against the walls.

No people.

Fun and fanciful weren't the first descriptions that came

to mind. The grass around the cabins, though, was green and clipped short. Someone took the trouble to maintain it all.

If only she could find that person.

Or people. She prayed for people.

The view spread before her was a glorious patchwork of golden grasses, khaki gum trees and a flash of silver river, all haloed and in soft focus from the late-afternoon sunshine. Josie had to fight back the absurd desire to cry.

What on earth had Marty and Frank been thinking?

You were the one who said you wanted some peace and quiet, she reminded herself, collapsing on the top step and propping her chin in her hands.

Yes, but there was peace and quiet and then there was this.

From the front veranda of the cottage, there wasn't another habitation in sight. She hid her face in her hands. Marty and Frank knew her well enough to know she hadn't meant this, didn't they?

Her insides clenched and she pulled her hands away. She didn't want the kind of peace and quiet that landed a person so far from civilisation they couldn't get a signal on their cell-phone.

She wanted people. She wanted to lie back, close her eyes and hear people laughing and living. She wanted to watch people laughing and living. She wanted—

Enough already! This was the one nice thing Marty and Frank had done for her in…

She tried to remember, but her mind went blank. OK, so maybe they weren't the most demonstrative of brothers, but sending her on holiday was a nice thing. Did she intend spoiling it with criticisms and rank ingratitude?

Some people would kill to be in her position. Lots of people would love to spend a month in the gorgeous

Upper Hunter Valley of rural New South Wales with nothing to do.

She gazed about her wistfully. She wished all those people were lining the hills of this valley right now.

She dusted off her hands and pushed to her feet. She'd make the best of it. According to her map there was a town a few kilometres further on. She could drive in there whenever she wanted. She'd make friends. She was tired. That was all. It had taken too long to get here, which was probably why her landlord had given up on her.

She wondered what kind of people would live out here all on their own. Hopefully the kind of people who took a solitary soul under their wing, introduced them around and enthusiastically outlined all the local activities available. Hopefully they'd love a chat over a cup of tea and a biscuit.

Josie would provide the biscuits.

Impatience shifted through her. She rolled her shoulders, stamped her feet and gulped in a breath of late-afternoon air. She didn't recognise the dry, dusty scents she pulled into her lungs, so different from the humid, salt-laden air of Buchanan's Point on the coast, her home. Her stomach clenched up again at the unfamiliarity.

She didn't belong here.

'Nonsense.' She tried to laugh away the fanciful notion, but a great yearning for home welled inside her. The greyness settled more securely around her. She hastened down the three steps and back along the gravel path, hoping movement would give her thoughts new direction. She swung one way then another. She could check around the back, she supposed. Her landlord could be working in a…shed or vegetable plot or something.

In her hunger to clap eyes on a friendly face, Josie rushed around the side of the house to open the gate. Her fingers fumbled with the latch. Need ballooned inside her, a need for companionship, a need to connect with someone. The gate finally swung back to reveal a neat garden. Again, no flower beds or pots broke the austerity, but the lawn here too was clipped and short, the edges so precise they looked as if they'd been trimmed using a set square.

The fence was painted white to match the house and the obligatory rotary clothes-line sat smack-bang in the middle of it all. An old-fashioned steel one like the one Josie had at home. Its prosaic familiarity reassured her. She stared at the faded jeans, blue chambray shirt and navy boxer shorts hanging from it and decided her landlord must be male.

Why hadn't she found out his name from Marty or Frank? Although everything had moved so fast. They'd popped this surprise on her last night and had insisted on seeing her off at the crack of dawn this morning. Mrs Pengilly's bad turn, though, had put paid to an early start. Josie bit her lip. Maybe she should've stayed and—

A low, vicious growl halted her in her tracks. Icy fingers shot down her back and across her scalp.

Please God, no.

There hadn't been a 'Beware of the Dog' sign on the gate. She'd have seen it. She paid attention to those things. Close attention.

The growl came again, followed by the owner of the growl, and Josie's heart slugged so hard against her ribs she thought it might dash itself to pieces before the dog got anywhere near her. Her knees started to shake.

'Nice doggy,' she tried, but her tongue stuck to the

roof of her mouth, slurring her words and making them unintelligible.

The dog growled in answer. Nuh-uh, it wasn't a nice doggy and, although it wasn't as large as a Rottweiler or a Dobermann, it was heavy-set and its teeth, when bared, looked as vicious as if it were. She could imagine how easily those teeth would tear flesh.

She took a step back. The dog took a step forward.

She stopped. It stopped.

Her heart pounded so hard it hurt. She wanted to buckle over but she refused to drop her eyes from the dog's glare. It lowered its head and showed its teeth again. All the hackles on its back lifted.

Ooh. Not a good sign. Everything inside Josie strained towards the gate and freedom, but she knew she wouldn't make it. The dog would be on her before she was halfway there. And those teeth…

Swallowing, she took another step back. The dog stayed put.

Another step. The dog didn't move. Its hackles didn't lower.

With a half-sob, Josie flung herself sideways and somehow managed to half climb, half pull her way up until she was sitting on top of the rotary clothes-line.

'Help!' she hollered at the top of her voice.

Something tickled her face. She lifted a hand to brush it away. Spider web! She tried to claw it off but it stuck with clammy tentacles to her face and neck. It was the last straw. Josie burst into tears.

The dog took up position directly beneath her. Lifting its head, it howled. It made Josie cry harder.

'What the devil—?'

A person. 'Thank you, God.' Finally, a friendly face. She swung towards the voice, almost falling off the clothes-line in relief.

She stared.

Her heart all but stopped.

Then it dropped clean out of her chest to lie gasping and flailing on the ground like a dying fish. *This was her friendly face?*

No!

Fresh sobs shook her. The dog started up its mournful howl again.

'For the love of…'

The man glared at her, shifted his feet, hands on hips. Nice lean hips she couldn't help noticing.

'Why in the dickens are you crying?'

She'd give up the sight of those lean hips and taut male thighs for a single smile.

He didn't smile. She stared at the hard, rocky crags of his face and doubted this man could do friendly. He didn't have a single friendly feature on his face. Not one. Not even a tiny little one. The flint of his eyes didn't hold a speck of softness or warmth. She bet dickens wasn't the term he wanted to use either.

Heaven help her. This wasn't the kind of man who'd take her under his wing. A hysterical bubble rose in her throat. 'You're my landlord?'

His eyes narrowed. 'Are you Josephine Peterson?'

She nodded.

'Yes.' He scowled. 'I'm Kent Black.'

He didn't offer his hand, which she had to admit might be difficult considering she was stuck up his clothes-line.

'I asked why you were crying.'

Coming from another person the question would've been sympathetic, but not from Kent Black. Anyway, she'd have thought a more pressing question was 'What the dickens are you doing in my clothes-line?'

'Well?' He shifted again on those long, lean legs.

An hysterical bubble burst right out of her mouth. 'Why am I crying?' She bet he thought she was a madwoman.

'Yes.' His lips cracked open to issue the one curt word then closed over again.

'Why am I crying?' Her voice rose an octave. 'I'll tell you why I'm crying. I'm crying because, well look at this place.' She lifted her hands. 'It's the end of the earth,' She fixed him with a glare. It was the only thing that stopped her from crying again. 'How could Marty and Frank think I'd want to come here, huh?'

'Look, Ms Peterson, I think you ought to calm—'

'Oh, no, you don't. You asked the question and demanded an answer so you can darn well listen to it.' She pointed her finger at him as if he was personally responsible for everything that had gone wrong today.

'Not only am I stuck here at the end of the earth but…but I'm stuck in a clothes-line at the end of the earth. And to rub salt into the wound, I got lost trying to find this rotten place and ended up in Timbuktu, where I got a flat tyre. Then your dog chased me up this rotten clothes-line and there's spider web everywhere!'

Her voice rose with each word in a way that appalled her, but she couldn't rein it back the way she normally did. 'And Mrs Pengilly took a bad turn this morning and I had to call an ambulance and…and I buried my father a fortnight ago and…'

Her anger ran out. Just like that. She closed her eyes and

dropped her head. 'And I miss him,' she finished on a whisper so soft she hardly heard it herself.

Darn it. She reluctantly opened one eye and found him staring at her as if she was a madwoman. She opened the other eye and straightened. Then smoothed down her hair. She wasn't a madwoman. And despite her outburst she didn't feel much like apologising either. He didn't have the kind of face that invited apologies. She pulled in a breath and met his gaze.

'You're afraid of my dog?'

She raised an eyebrow. Did he think she sat in clothes-lines for the fun of it? 'Even at the end of the earth you should put signs up on your gates warning people about vicious dogs.'

He continued to survey her with that flinty gaze and she felt herself redden beneath it. With a sigh, she lifted her T-shirt. She didn't need to glance down to see the jagged white scar that ran the length of her right side and across her stomach. She could trace it in her dreams. To do him credit, though, he hardly blinked.

'How old were you?'

'Twelve.'

'And you're afraid of Molly here?'

Wasn't that obvious?

She glanced at the dog. Molly? The name wasn't right up there with Killer or Slasher or Crusher, was it? And with Kent Black standing beside her the dog didn't look anywhere near as formidable as it had a moment ago. Josie gulped. 'She's a girl?'

'Yep.'

The dog that had attacked her had been a big male Dobermann. 'She growled at me.'

'You frightened her.'

'Me?' She nearly fell out of the clothes-line.

'If you'd clapped your hands and said boo she'd have run away.'

Now she really didn't believe him.

His lips twisted, but not into a smile. 'Moll.' The dog wagged her tail and shuffled across to him. He scratched her behind the ears. 'Roll over, girl.'

His voice was low and gentle and it snagged at Josie's insides. Molly rolled onto her back and a part of Josie didn't blame her. If he spoke to her like that she'd roll over too.

Oh, don't be so ridiculous, she ordered. She focused her attention back on Kent. He parted the fur on the dog's belly. He had large, weathered hands. Even from her perch in the clothes-line she could see the calluses that lined his fingers.

'Look,' he ordered.

She did, and saw a mirror image of her own scar etched in the dog's flesh. An ugly white raised scar that jagged across Molly's stomach and ribs.

'A man with a piece of four-by-two studded with nails did that to her.'

Sympathy and horror pounded through Josie in equal measure. How could someone hurt a defenceless animal like that? It was inhuman.

She scrambled down out of the clothes-line, dropped to her knees at its base and held out her arms. 'You poor thing.'

Molly walked straight into them.

Kent had never seen anything like it in all his thirty-two years. Molly hid from strangers. When someone surprised her, like Josephine Peterson here obviously had, she'd try and bluff her way out of it by growling and stalking off.

Then she'd hide. The one thing she didn't do was let strangers pet her. She sure as hell didn't let them hug her.

For the first time in a long time Kent found himself wanting to smile. Then he remembered Josephine Peterson's blood-curdling cry for help and he went cold all over again. He didn't need a woman like her at Eagle Reach.

A woman who couldn't look after herself.

He'd bet each and every one of his grass-fed steers that Josephine Peterson didn't have a self-sufficient bone in her body. And he'd be blowed if he'd take on the role of her protector.

His lip curled. She was a mouse. She had mousy brown hair, mousy brown eyes and a mouse-thin body that looked as if it'd bow under the weight of an armload of firewood. Even her smile was all mousiness—timid and tentative. She aimed it at him now, but he refused to return it.

It trembled right off her lips. Guilt slugged him in the guts. He bit back an oath.

She rose and cast a fearful glance at the back of the house. 'Do…do you have any other dogs?'

'No.' The memory of her scarred abdomen rushed on him again. His hands clenched to fists. When she'd lifted her shirt, shown him her scar, it wasn't tenderness or desire that had surged through him. He had a feeling, though, that it was something closely related, something partway between the two, something he didn't have a name for.

What he did know was he didn't want Josephine Peterson here on his hill. She didn't belong here. She was a townie, a city girl. For Pete's sake, look at her fingernails. Long and perfectly painted in a shimmery pink. They were squared off at the tips with such uniformity he knew they had to be fake. This wasn't fake-fingernail country.

It was roughing-it country.

He hadn't seen anyone less likely to want to rough it than Josephine Peterson.

When he glanced at her again she tried another smile. 'Do you have a wife?'

Her soft question slammed into him with more force than it had any right to. She needn't look to him for that either!

He glanced into her hopeful face and despite his best intentions desire fired along his nerve-endings, quickening his blood, reminding him of everything he'd turned his back on. Now that she stood directly in front of him, rather than perched up in his clothes-line or on her knees with her face buried in Molly's fur, he could see the gold flecks inside the melt-in-your-mouth chocolate of her iris. That didn't look too mousy.

Get a grip! Whatever the colour of her eyes, it didn't change the fact she wasn't the kind of woman he went for. He'd been stuck up this hill too long. He liked tall, curvy blondes who were out for a good time and nothing more. Josephine Peterson wasn't tall, curvy or blonde. And she looked too earnest for the kind of no-strings affairs he occasionally indulged in.

She continued to gaze at him hopefully. 'No,' he bit out. 'I don't have a wife.' And he had no intention of landing himself with one either. The sooner this woman realised that the better.

Rather than light up with interest, with calculation, her face fell. Kent did a double take.

'That's a shame. It would've been nice to have a woman around to talk to.'

He'd have laughed out loud at his mistake only he'd lost his funny bone.

'Is there anyone else here besides you?'

'No.' He snapped the word out. 'I'll get the key to your cabin.'

She blinked at his abruptness. 'Which one is mine?'

'They're all empty.' He strode around to the back of his house. She had to run to keep up with him. With a supreme effort he slowed his stride. 'You can have your pick.'

'I'll take that one.'

She pointed to the nearest cabin and Kent found himself biting back another oath. Damn and blast. Why hadn't he put her in the furthest one and been done with it? He disappeared inside, seized the key then strode back outside and thrust it at her.

'Thank…thank you. Umm…' She shuffled from one foot to the other. 'Does the cabin have a phone?'

His lip curled. He despised city folk. They came here mouthing clichés proclaiming they wanted to get away from it all, get back to nature, but all hell broke loose when they discovered they had to do without their little luxuries. It made him sick.

Granted, though, Josephine Peterson looked as though she wanted to be at Eagle Reach about as much as he wanted her here. Her earlier words came back to him and a laugh scraped out of his throat. 'This is the end of the earth, remember? What do you think?'

She eyed him warily. The gold in her eyes glittered. 'I'm guessing that's a no.'

'You're guessing right.'

She wouldn't last a month. At this rate she'd be lucky to last two days. What on earth had possessed her to book a cabin for four whole weeks? The advertisement he'd placed in the local tourism rag made no false promises. It sure as hell wasn't the kind of advert designed to attract the attention of the likes of her.

'Look, Ms Peterson, this obviously isn't your cup of tea. Why don't you go on into Gloucester? It's only half an hour further on. You'll find accommodation more suited to your tastes there.' Behind his back he crossed his fingers. 'I'll even return your deposit.'

'Please, call me Josie.'

She paused as if waiting for him to return the favour and tell her to call him Kent, but he had no intention of making any friendly overtures. He wanted her out of here.

When he remained silent, she sighed. 'I have to stay. My brothers organised all this as a treat.'

He recalled her rant whilst she'd clung to his clothes-line. Marty and Frank, wasn't it? His eyes narrowed. 'Are they practical jokers?'

'Heavens, no.' For a moment she looked as if she might laugh. It faded quickly. 'Which is why I have to stay. I wouldn't hurt their feelings for the world. And they would be hurt if they found out I'd stayed some-where else.'

Fabulous.

She smiled then. He recognised the effort behind it, and its simple courage did strange things to his insides. He wanted to resist it. Instinct warned him against befriend-ing this woman.

'Is Gloucester where I'll find the nearest phone? It's just...I'm not getting a signal on my mobile.'

Which was one of the reasons he loved this hill.

'And I'd really like to check on my neighbour, Mrs Pengilly.'

For a mouse she could sure make him feel like a heel.

'There's a phone in there.' He hitched his head in the direction of the house.

Josie's face lit up. 'May I...?'

'It's in the kitchen.'

She raced inside as if afraid he'd take his offer back. He collapsed onto the top step, shoulders sagging, and tried not to overhear her conversation, tried not to hear how she assured whoever answered the phone that the Gloucester Valley was beautiful, that the view from her cabin was glorious, that her cabin was wonderful.

He leapt up and started to pace. Two out of three wasn't bad. The Gloucester Valley *was* beautiful, and her view *was* glorious. He had a feeling she'd give up both for the wonderful cabin.

He blinked when she reappeared moments later. He'd expected her to be on the phone for hours. It was what women did, wasn't it?

She tripped down the back steps. 'Thank you, I...' She made as if to clasp his arm then stepped back as though she'd thought better of it. 'Thank you.'

His pulse quickened. 'How's your Mrs Pengilly?'

He couldn't believe he'd asked. Maybe it was time he had a holiday.

A smile lit her face. 'Her son Jacob came down from Brisbane and he says she's going to be OK. Apparently she has late-onset diabetes.'

'Once they've stabilised her blood sugar and organised her medication she'll be fine.' The words rolled out of him with an ease that was disconcerting.

'Yes.' The gold of her eyes glittered with curiosity. 'You sound like you know all about it.'

'I do.' But he wasn't volunteering any more information.

He'd already given enough away. He reached across and plucked the key from her fingers. 'Let's get you settled.'

To Josie, Kent's words sounded more like 'Let's get you out of my hair'. Nope, not a friendly bone in his body.

He did have a nice body, though—broad-shouldered, lean-hipped, athletic. And he wasn't all bad. He had let her use his phone. And he'd asked after Mrs Pengilly.

She trotted to keep up with him. She glanced at him from the corner of her eye and noted the uncompromising line of his mouth. Maybe he was just out of practice. Living here all on his own, he wouldn't get much chance at personable conversation. Anyhow, she was determined to give him the benefit of the doubt because the alternative was too bleak for words—stuck out in the middle of nowhere with a man who wouldn't give her the time of day.

No. No. She bit back a rising tide of panic. Beneath his gruffness Kent had a kind heart.

On what proof are you basing such an assumption? a disbelieving voice at the back of her head demanded.

She swallowed. He'd asked after an old lady. And… And he had a dog.

Not much though, is it? the same voice pointed out with maddening logic.

No, she guessed not. The panic rose through her again. 'Did you nurse Molly back to health?'

'Yes.'

One uncompromising word, but it lifted the weight settling across her shoulders. See? He did have a kind heart. For dogs.

It was a start.

Kent leapt up onto the tiny veranda that fronted the

cabin and pushed the key into the door. Josie started after him then swallowed. The cabins all looked really tiny. She'd hoped…

The door swung open and she gulped back a surge of disappointment. When Marty and Frank had said 'cabin' she'd thought… Well, she hadn't expected five-star luxury or anything, but she had hoped for three-star comfort.

She was landed with one-star basic. And that was being charitable.

Kent's shoulders stiffened as if he sensed her judgement and resented it. 'It has everything you need.' He pointed. 'The sofa pulls out into a bed.'

Uh-huh. She took a tentative step into the room and glanced around. Where were the flowers? The bowl of fruit? The welcoming bottle of bubbly? There wasn't a single rug on the floor or print on the wall. No colourful throw on the sofa either. In fact, there wasn't a throw full stop, grey or otherwise.

Admittedly, everything looked clean, scrubbed to within an inch of its life. By the light of the single overhead bulb—no light shade—the table and two chairs gleamed dully. Would it really have been such an effort to toss over a tablecloth and tie on chair pads?

'The kitchen is fully equipped.'

It was. It had an oven and hotplates, a toaster and kettle. But it didn't have any complimentary sachets of tea or coffee. It didn't have a dishwasher. She hadn't wanted the world, but—

An awful thought struck her. 'Is there a bathroom?'

Without a word, Kent strode forward and opened a door she hadn't noticed in the far wall. She wasn't sure she wanted to look.

She ordered her legs forward, glanced through the door and released the breath she held. There was a flushable toilet. And a shower.

But no bathtub.

So much for the aromatherapy candles and scented bath oils she'd packed.

'What do you think?'

Josie gaped at him. The question seemed so out of character she found herself blurting out her first impression without restraint. 'It's awful.'

He stiffened as if she'd slapped him.

'I'm sorry, I don't mean to offend you, but it's a dog kennel.' In fact, she bet Molly's quarters surpassed this. 'It's… Do all the cabins have the same colour scheme?'

The pulse at the base of his jaw jerked. 'What's wrong with the colour scheme?'

'It's grey!' Couldn't he see that? Did he seriously think grey made for a homely, inspiring atmosphere? A holiday atmosphere?

He folded his arms. His eyes glittered. 'All the cabins are identical.'

So she was stuck with it, then.

'Look, I know this probably isn't up to your usual standard,' he unfolded his arms, 'but I only promised basic accommodation and—'

'It doesn't matter.' Tiredness surged through her. Was this all Marty and Frank thought she was worth? She gulped back the lump in her throat.

'Like you said, it has everything I need.' The greyness settled behind her eyelids.

CHAPTER TWO

KENT strode off into the lengthening shadows of the afternoon, his back stiff, his jaw clenched. For once he didn't
notice the purple-green goldness of the approaching sunset.
He skidded to a halt, spun around and slapped a hand to
his thigh. 'C'mon, Moll.'

Molly pricked her ears forward, thumped her tail against
the rough-hewn boards of the cabin's veranda, but she
didn't move from her post by Josie's door.

Oh, great. Just great.

'See if I care,' he muttered, stalking back off. Solitude
was his preferred state of affairs. Josie Peterson was
welcome to his dog for all the good it would do her. Molly
wouldn't say boo to a fly.

Birds of a feather…

Up on the ridge a kookaburra started its boisterous cry
and in the next moment the hills were ringing with answering laughter. Kent ground to a halt. He swung back in frustration, hands on hips.

These cabins weren't meant for the likes of her. They
were meant for men like him. And for men who lived in
cities and hungered to get away occasionally, even if only
for a long weekend. Men who wanted to leave the stench

of car exhaust fumes and smog and crowds and endless traffic behind. Men who wanted nothing more than to see the sky above their heads, breathe fresh air into their lungs, and feel grass rather than concrete beneath their feet. Men happy to live on toast and tea and beer for three days.

Josie didn't want that. She'd want spa baths and water-beds. She'd want seafood platters and racks of lamb and soft, woody chardonnays.

And he didn't blame her. If she'd just lost her father she probably deserved some pampering, a treat, not this rugged emptiness. Her brothers had to be certifiable idiots.

He kicked at a stone. He couldn't give her spa baths and seafood platters.

A vivid image of mousy Josie Peterson lying back in a bubble-filled spa rose up through him and his skin went tight. She didn't look too mousy in that fantasy.

He scratched a hand through his hair. Idiot. The kookaburras continued to laugh. Their derision itched through him. He surveyed the cabin, hands on hips. Not a sign of movement. His earlier vision gave way to one of her lying face down on the sofa, sobbing. He took a step towards the cabin.

He ground to a halt.

He didn't do crying women. Not any more.

A month. *A whole month.*

His gaze flicked to her car. He wasn't a blasted porter either, but that didn't stop him from stalking over to it and removing two suitcases and a box of groceries. Or from stalking back to the house, grabbing a bottle of chardonnay and shoving it in an ice bucket and adding that to the items piled up by her front door.

He bent down and scratched Molly's ears. 'Keep an eye

on her, girl.' That would have to do. Common decency demanded he check on her in the morning, then his neighbourly duty was done.

If she hadn't already had a crying jag when perched in the clothes-line, Josie would've had one now. But she decided one a day was enough.

A whole month. She was stuck out here for a whole month. *On her own.*

She tried to repress a shudder. She tried to force herself to smile as she glanced around the interior of the cabin again. She'd read somewhere that if you smiled it actually helped lift your spirits.

Ha! Not working.

She scrubbed her hands down her face. Oh, well, she supposed if nothing else she at least had plenty of time to sort out what she was going to do with the rest of her life. And that was the point of this holiday after all.

Things inside her cringed and burned. She wrapped her arms around her waist. She wasn't qualified to do anything other than look after sick people. And she didn't want to do that any more.

Familiar doubts and worries crowded in on her. She pushed them away. Later. She'd deal with them later.

With a sigh, she collapsed onto the sofa. Then groaned. It was as rock-hard as Kent Black. That didn't bode well. She twisted against it, trying to get comfortable. It didn't take a brain surgeon to work out Kent didn't want her here. As far as she could see, he didn't have an ounce of sympathy in that big, broad body of his for weakness of any kind.

She had to admit it was a nice, broad body though, with scrummy shoulders. If a girl disregarded that scowl she could get all sorts of ideas in her head and—

No, she couldn't! Besides, Josie could never disregard that scowl. Kent didn't think she belonged out here and he was one hundred per cent right.

A whole month.

'Stop it!'

Her voice echoed eerily in the cabin, reminding her how alone she was. She suppressed another shudder. She was just tired, that was all, and sitting around wallowing in self-pity wasn't going to help. A shower, that was what she needed. That'd pep her up. Then she'd unpack the car and make a cup of tea. Things always looked better over a cup of tea.

The shower did help. She emerged into the main room of the cabin, vigorously drying her hair. Then froze.

Something was on her veranda!

There it was again. A scuffling, creaking, snorting noise right outside her front door. She hadn't locked it!

Josie's mouth went dry. She held the towel to her face. Oh, please. Whatever was out there she prayed it didn't have an opposable thumb, that it couldn't reach out and open door handles.

And that it didn't have the kind of bulk that barged through flimsy wooden doors.

Just clap your hands and say boo!

Kent's earlier advice almost made her laugh out loud. Not funny ha-ha, but losing it big-time ha-ha. She retreated to the bathroom door. She doubted she could manage much of a boo at the moment.

'Kent?' Maybe he was out there. Maybe he'd come back for... She couldn't think of any conceivable reason why he'd come back. He hadn't been able to get away fast enough, horrible, unfriendly man.

She'd give anything for it to be him out there now, though. 'Mr Black?'

A low whine answered her, followed by scratching at her door and a bark.

'Molly.' With her heart hammering in her throat, Josie stumbled forward, wrenched the door open and dropped to her knees to hug the dog. 'You scared me half out of my wits,' she scolded. Molly licked her face in response.

Thank heavens Kent hadn't been here to witness her panic. He'd have laughed his head off then curled his lip in scorn. She'd have died on the spot.

She glanced out into the darkness and gulped. Night had fallen in full force. She couldn't remember a night so dark. Not a single streetlight pierced the blackness. Her cabin faced away from Kent's house, so not a single house light penetrated it either. The moon hadn't risen yet, but a multitude of stars arced across the sky in a display that hitched the breath in her throat.

She should've unpacked her car whilst it was light. She didn't fancy stumbling around in the dark. Dragging her eyes from the glory of the night sky, she turned and found her suitcases lined up neatly on the end of her veranda. Her jaw dropped. Kent had unpacked her car for her?

That was nice. Friendly. In fact—she struggled to her feet—it was almost…sweet?

No, you couldn't describe Kent as sweet.

She reached for the nearest bag then stilled. She adjusted her reach to the right and picked up an ice bucket, complete with a bottle of wine.

She blinked madly and hugged it to her chest. Now, that *was* friendly.

And sweet. Most definitely sweet.

* * *

Josie groaned and pulled a pillow over her head in an effort to drown out the cacophony of noise. Molly whined and scratched to be let out. She'd spent the night sleeping on the end of the sofa bed, and Josie had welcomed the company. Molly's presence had made her feel less alone. Last night she'd needed that.

Now she needed sleep.

Molly whined again. Groaning, Josie reached for her watch. Six o'clock! She crawled out of bed and opened the door. Kookaburras laughed as if the sight of her filled them with hilarity and, overhead, white cockatoos screeched, three crows adding their raucous caws. And that wasn't counting all the other cheeps and peeps and twitters she didn't recognise in the general riot. Magpies started warbling in a nearby gum tree. For heaven's sake, what was this place—a bird sanctuary?

Flashes of red and green passed directly in front of her to settle in a row of nearby grevillias, twittering happily as they supped on red-flowered nectar. Rosellas. Ooh. She loved rosellas.

Racing back inside, she clicked on the kettle, pulled on her jeans, threw on a shirt then dashed back out to her veranda with a steaming mug of coffee to watch as the world woke up around her.

OK. So maybe Eagle Reach was at the end of the earth, but she couldn't deny its beauty. To her left, the row of grevillias, still covered in rosellas, merged into a forest of gums and banksias. To her right, the five other cabins stretched away down the slope. Directly in front of her the hill fell away in gentle folds, the grassy slopes golden in the early-morning sunlight, dazzled with dew.

She blinked at its brightness, the freshness. Moist earth

and sun-warmed grasses and the faint tang of eucalyptus scented the air. She gulped it in greedily.

In the distance the River Gloucester, lined with river gums and weeping willows, wound its way along the base of the hill to disappear behind a neighbouring slope. Josie knew that if she followed the river she would eventually come to the little township of Martin's Gully, and then, further along, the larger township of Gloucester itself.

As one, the rosellas lifted from the bushes and took flight and, just like that, Josie found herself alone again. She swallowed. What would she find to do all day? Especially in light of the resolution she'd made last night.

She chafed her hands. She'd think of something. She'd stay at Eagle Reach for the whole day if it killed her. She would not drive into either Martin's Gully or Gloucester. Kent Black would expect her to do exactly that. And for some reason she found herself wanting to smash his expectations.

She found herself aching for just an ounce of his strength too.

By eight o'clock Josie wondered again at the sense of such a resolution. She'd breakfasted, tidied the cabin and now...

Nothing.

She made another coffee and sat back out on the veranda. She checked her watch. Five past eight. Even if she went to bed disgustingly early she still had at least twelve hours to kill. Her shoulders started to sag and her spine lost its early-morning buoyancy, the greyness of grief descending over her again.

She shouldn't have come here. It was too soon for a holiday. Any holiday. She'd buried her father a fortnight ago. She should be at home. She should be with her friends, her family. Maybe, right at this very minute, she could be forging closer bonds with Marty and Frank. Surely that was more important than—

'Good morning!'

Josie jumped out of her skin. Coffee sloshed over the side of her cup and onto her feet. Kent Black. Her heart hammered, though she told herself it was the effect of her fright. Not the fact that his big, broad body looked superb in a pair of faded jeans and a navy T-shirt that fitted him in a way that highlighted bulging arm muscles.

'Sorry. Didn't mean to startle you.'

He didn't look the least bit sorry. And if he didn't mean to startle people he shouldn't bark out good-mornings like a sergeant major springing a surprise inspection.

'Not a problem.' She tried to smile. 'Good morning.'

He didn't step any closer, he didn't come and sit with her on the veranda. She quelled her disappointment and tried to tell herself she didn't care.

'How'd you sleep?' The words scraped out of a throat that sounded rusty with disuse.

'Like a top,' she lied. She decided she'd been rude enough about the amenities—or lack of amenities—last night. She couldn't start back in on him today. Yesterday at least she could plead the excuse of tiredness. 'I'm sorry about my lack of enthusiasm last night. It had been a long day and, like you said, the cabin is perfectly adequate.'

He blinked. His eyes narrowed. Up close she could see they were the most startling shade of blue, almost navy. Still, it didn't mean she wanted them practically dissecting her.

'How was the wine?'

A smile spread through her. He could look as unfriendly and unapproachable as he liked, but actions spoke louder than words. Last night, over her first glass of wine, she'd decided Kent Black had a kind heart. He'd just forgotten how to show it, that was all. 'The wine was lovely.'

Really lovely. So lovely she'd drunk half the bottle before she'd realised it. Once she had, she'd hastily shoved the rest of the bottle in the tiny bar fridge. Quaffing copious quantities of wine when she was stuck out here all on her own might not be the wisest of ideas.

'It was a really thoughtful gesture. Thank you, Mr Black.' She waited for him to tell her to call him Kent. She bit back a sigh when he didn't.

He touched the brim of his hat in what she took to be a kind of farewell salute and panic spiked through her. She didn't want to be left all alone again. Not yet.

Molly nudged Josie's arm with her nose, forcing her to lift it so she could sidle in close. 'I, umm… Molly is a lovely dog. Really lovely. I was wrong about her too.' Ugh, she should be ashamed of such inane babble. 'I… She spent the night with me.'

He spun back, hands on hips. 'I noticed.'

Oh, dear. She should've let him leave. Her fingers curled into Molly's fur. She didn't want to give Molly up. 'I… Do you want me to shoo her home in future?'

'She's all yours.'

Relief chugged through her and she swore his eyes softened. Then he turned away again and she knew she must've imagined it. 'Are any of the other cabins booked over the next few weeks?' She crossed her fingers.

His impatience, when he turned back, made her want to cringe.

'No.'

The single syllable rang a death knell through her last

forlorn hope. All alone. For a month. 'Then…what do people do out here?'

'Do?' One eyebrow lifted. 'Nothing. That's the point.'

Dread fizzed through her. 'Would you like a cup of tea?' Surely he'd like a cup of tea. Kind hearts and cups of tea went together and—

'No.'

She gulped. Couldn't he have at least added a thank-you to his refusal? She tried to dredge up indignation, but her loneliness overrode it.

'Some of us actually have work to do.'

Work? 'What kind of work?' Could she help? She knew she was grasping at straws, but she couldn't stop herself. She knew she'd die a thousand deaths when she went back over this conversation later.

'I run cattle on this hill, Ms Peterson.'

'Josie,' she whispered, a hand fluttering to her throat. 'Please call me Josie.'

He pulled the brim of his hat down low over his eyes. 'Bushwalking.'

'I beg your pardon?'

'People who come here. They like to bushwalk.'

'Oh. OK.' She liked walking. She walked on the beach back home. She didn't know her way around here, though. What if she got lost? Who'd know she was missing? She didn't trust Kent Black to notice.

'There are some pretty trails through there.' He pointed at the forest of gums. 'They lead down to the river.'

Trails? She brightened. She could follow a path without getting lost.

'Take Molly with you.'

'OK. Thank you,' she called out after him, but she

doubted he'd heard. His long legs had already put an alarming amount of distance between them in a seriously short space of time.

She turned her gaze to the shadowed depths of the eucalypt forest and made out the beginnings of a path. A walk? She leapt up, glad to have a purpose.

Kent swung around as an almighty screech pierced the forest. Birds lifted from trees and fluttered away. He glanced at his watch and shook his head. Fifteen minutes. She'd lasted fifteen minutes. Not that he'd deliberately followed her, of course. He hadn't. He'd just taken note of when she'd set off and down which path, that was all.

He'd chosen a different path, an adjacent one, and it wasn't as if he was keeping an eye on her or anything. He had business down this way.

Yeah, but not until later this afternoon, a voice in his head jeered

He ignored it.

No more screams or screeches or shrieks for help followed. She'd probably walked into a spider's web or something. But then Molly started up her low, mournful howl. Kent folded his arms and glared. With a muttered curse, he unfolded his arms, cut through the undergrowth and set off towards the noise.

He almost laughed out loud when he reached them. Josie clung to a branch of a nearby gum and a goanna clung to the main trunk of the same tree, effectively cutting off her escape. Molly sat beneath it all, howling for all she was worth. He chuckled then realised what he'd done.

'Enjoying your walk I hope, Ms Peterson?'

She swung her head around to glare at him over her

shoulder. The branch swayed precariously. He readied himself to catch her if she overbalanced.

'What do you think?' she snapped.

'I think you enjoy scaring all the wildlife on my side of the hill.'

'Scaring? Me?' Her mouth opened and closed but no sound came out. She pointed an accusing finger at the goanna then clutched the branch again as it started to sway. 'Move it.'

He glanced at it. 'Nope, not touching it.'

'So, you're scared of it too?' she hissed.

'Let's just say I like to treat our native wildlife with a great deal of respect.'

'Oh, that's just great. Of all the wildlife in this God-forsaken place I had to get a…a dinosaur rather than a cute, cuddly koala, huh? Any wildlife wrestlers in the neighbourhood by any chance?'

'Not much call for them out here.'

'How am I going to get down?'

Behind her bluff he could see she was scared. He had a feeling she hadn't stopped being scared since she'd scrambled out of his clothes-line yesterday. 'Jump,' he ordered. 'I'll catch you.' She wasn't that high up. In fact, if she hung from that branch by her hands, she'd only be four or five feet from the ground. He knew it would look vastly different from her perspective, though.

He wished she wasn't so cute.

The thought flitted in and out of his head in the time it took to blink. 'Cut out the racket, Molly,' he growled. The dog had kept right on howling all this time. Like most of the females of his experience, Molly loved the sound of her own voice.

Josie bit her lip and glanced at the goanna. 'Is it going to jump too? Or chase me?'

'Nope. This is his tree. It's where he feels safe.'

She glared at him again. 'So, of all the trees in the forest I had to pick his?'

'Yep.'

'I'm so happy.'

He guessed from the way she gritted her teeth together as she said it, she didn't mean it.

Without any more prompting on his part, Josie shifted her weight from her behind to her stomach then tried to take her full weight with her arms to lower herself to the ground. Kent leapt forward and wrapped his arms around the tops of her thighs.

'I don't need—'

The rest of her words were lost when her hands slipped and she landed against him with a muffled, 'Oomph.'

Kent couldn't manage much either as the top half of her body slumped over him and he found his face mashed between her breasts. Then a long, delicious slide as her body slipped down his.

They were both breathing hard when her feet finally touched the ground.

They paused then sprang apart.

'Thank you,' Josie babbled, smoothing down her hair. 'I, umm… It probably wasn't necessary to jump to my rescue like that, but, umm…thank you all the same.'

'Are you going to make a habit of that?' he snapped. He darn well hoped not. His body wouldn't cope with it. Even now he had to fight down a rising tide of raw desire. He didn't need this.

'It's not part of my plans.'

He wanted her off his mountain. Fast. He flung his arms out. 'Doesn't this prove how unsuited you are to this place?'

Her chin shot up although her shoulders stayed hunched around her ears. 'Because I'm frightened of goannas?'

'Because you're frightened of everything.'

'I'm not afraid of Molly. Not now,' she pointed out reasonably enough. 'I just didn't know what to do when that thing started running at me.'

'Run away at right angles to it,' he answered automatically.

'I'll remember that.'

He didn't want her remembering. He wanted her gone. 'You don't know how to protect yourself out here.'

'Well…I'm not dead yet.'

'What would you do if some big, burly guy jumped out at you, huh?' To prove his point, he lunged at her.

The next moment he was lying on his back, and staring up through the leaves of the trees at the clear blue of the sky. With no idea how he had got there.

Josie's face hovered into view as she leaned over him. 'Does that answer your question?'

She'd thrown him? He deserved that smug little smile. For some reason he wanted to laugh again.

He scowled. No, he didn't. He wanted her off his mountain.

'I might be hopeless, but I'm not completely helpless, you know. Men I can defend myself against. It's the dogs and goannas that I have trouble with.'

He rolled over onto his stomach to watch her saunter away. He really wished he didn't notice how sweetly she filled out a pair of jeans. Molly licked his face, as if in sympathy, then trotted after her new-found friend.

CHAPTER THREE

JOSIE was back at her cabin by ten o'clock.

So, now she only had ten hours to kill.

She wished she'd learnt how to draw or paint. Or knit.

A craft project, that was what she needed. She made a mental note to hunt out a craft shop when she went into Gloucester. Tomorrow.

Still, what would it hurt if she went in today and—?

Kent's scornful lips flashed through her mind. No! She'd manage to stick it out here for a whole day. Somehow.

Books. She'd buy some books. And a radio. Tomorrow.

She rearranged her grocery supplies on the kitchen shelves. That took less than ten minutes. She made a shopping list. For tomorrow. That took another ten minutes, but only because she dallied over it. She glanced around, clapped her hands together and wondered what she could do next.

'Oh, for heaven's sake!' she growled out loud, suddenly impatient. Seizing a pen and notepad, she plonked herself down at the table. If she'd just work out what she wanted to do with the rest of her life instead of putting it off, then she could get on with living that life and leave this awful place behind. Marty and Frank would forgive her for curtailing her holiday if she came up with a plan.

At the top of the page she wrote: 'What do I want to do with my life?' Her mind went blank, so she added an exclamation mark, in brackets.

Familiar doubts and worries flitted about her. She swallowed and tried not to panic. She was looking at this all wrong. She should break it down into smaller, more manageable bits. Skills. She should list her skills.

1—Assistant in Nursing certificate. 2—She could give bed baths. 3—She could measure out medicines. 4—She could coax a difficult patient to eat. 5—

No. No. No.

She slammed the pen to the table. She didn't want to do those things any more. There had to be other things she could do. She had to have at least one talent that could steer her towards a new vocation. Take her brothers. Frank had a great head for figures, which made him a successful accountant. Marty had great spatial abilities, which was why he was an architect. She had...?

Nothing.

Her shoulders sagged. She couldn't think of one single thing she had a talent for. Except looking after sick people, dying people. Fear clogged her throat. She couldn't do that. Not any more. She'd loved her father dearly, missed him terribly, and she didn't regret one single day she'd spent looking after him. But...

She couldn't take on another dementia patient. She couldn't watch another person die.

She leapt up and started to pace. The grey drabness of the cabin pressed in against her. The only splashes of colour were the labels on her groceries. Her gaze drifted across them, paused on the packet cake mix that, for some reason, she'd thrown in. What? Did she think she'd be giving tea parties? Her laugh held an edge that earned her a low bark from Molly.

She'd love to give a tea party. A sigh welled up inside her. She chewed her bottom lip and cast another glance at the cake mix. She could cook it up for Kent.

As a thank-you for last night's bottle of wine.

Maybe he'd even invite her to stay and share it. She chewed her bottom lip some more. She wanted to find out what made him tick, what made him so strong. She wanted to be more like that. She put her list away and reached for a mixing bowl.

Kent rubbed his hands together as he waited for the tea to brew. With his chores done, he could kick back and enjoy the fading golden light of the afternoon, his favourite time of day.

The cattle were fed and watered. He ran a herd small enough to manage on his own. And between them, the cattle and the cabins, they kept him busy enough through the days.

The nights, though…

The nights nothing!

A knock sounded on his back door. He swung around. Josie?

It had to be. He rarely had visitors out here, which was the way he liked it. He wasn't a sociable man. He thought he'd made that plain to her this morning.

Guilt wormed through him. He scowled at the teapot.

Maybe she'd come to return the key and tell him she was leaving? His jaw clenched. Good. She could drive off into the sunset. He didn't care. No skin off his nose.

'Kent?' She knocked again.

He bit back a string of curses and strode out to answer the door. The sharp remark on his lips died when he found her standing on the bottom step with a frosted chocolate cake in her hands and a hopeful expression in her gold-flecked eyes.

Damn.

'Hello.' She smiled, or at least her lips gave the tiniest of upward lifts.

He grunted in reply. Things inside him shuffled about and refused to settle into place.

She'd recently showered and damp hair curled around her shoulders. It gleamed in the last shaft of sunlight that touched his house for the afternoon, and he could pick out more shades of brown than he thought possible for one person to possess. Everything from light honeyed brown all the way through to rich walnut.

And not a mouse in sight.

She smelled fresh and fruity. Not run-of-the-mill apples and oranges either, but something more exotic. Like pineapple and...cucumber? She smelt like summer nights on the beach.

He couldn't remember the last time he'd sat on a beach. Or when he'd last wanted to. He couldn't remember the last time he'd eaten chocolate cake either. He tried to stop his mouth from watering.

She thrust the cake towards him. 'This is for you.'

He had no option but to take it. 'Why?' His eyes narrowed. He didn't trust the sensations pounding through him and he didn't trust her either.

Her gaze darted behind him into the house. She moistened her lips when she met his gaze again. 'I, umm—'

'You want to use the phone again?' Typical woman. Couldn't be without—

'No.' She drew herself up. 'It's a thank-you for last night's bottle of wine.'

He'd known he'd end up regretting that bottle of wine. He stared at her. She had a pointy little chin that stuck out when indignant. He wanted to reach out a finger and trace the fine line of her jaw.

He darn well didn't! He shoved the cake back at her. 'I don't want it.'

She took a step back and blinked. Then amazingly she laughed. 'Wrong answer, Mr Black; you're supposed to say thank you.'

Shame bore down on him. There was a world of difference between unsociable and downright rude. Jeez. 'You're right.' He dragged his free hand down his face. 'I'm sorry.' He pulled in a breath and tried to gulp back hasty words clamouring for release. 'You better call me Kent.'

He couldn't grind back the rest of his words either.

'I've just made a pot of tea. Would you like to join me?'

The gold flecks in her eyes lit up. 'Yes, please.'

Josie wanted to run from Kent's scowl. Then she remembered the only place she could run to was her cabin. Her bleak, lonely cabin. She gulped back her trepidation and followed him into the kitchen.

She wrinkled her nose as she glanced around. Definitely a bachelor's pad—no frills, no colour, next to no comfort. A woman wouldn't put up with this.

She glanced at Kent. She had a feeling he wouldn't give two hoots what a woman thought.

A large wooden table dominated the room. That was about all she'd taken in yesterday when she'd made her quick phone call. She wondered if there was a separate dining room, then dismissed the idea. The house wasn't large enough.

She glanced through the doorway leading through to the rest of the house. It looked like a typical gun-barrel miner's cottage. The next room along would be the living room then a short hallway would lead to two bedrooms at the front of the house.

She also guessed she'd never make it past this kitchen.

Heat suddenly flamed through her. Not that she wanted to make it as far as the bedroom with Kent Black, of course. Good lord. She couldn't imagine him unbending his stiff upper lip long enough to kiss a woman, let alone—

Are you so sure? a wicked voice asked.

Umm…

She slammed a lid on that thought, swung away and found herself confronted with the hard, lean lines of Kent's back…and backside, as he reached into a cupboard above the sink for two mugs.

Oh, dear. She fanned her face and swung around another ninety degrees. She didn't want to ogle his, uh, assets. In fact, it probably wasn't a good idea to ogle any man's assets until she'd sorted out what she was going to do with the rest of her life.

The rest of her life? What was she going to do with the next ten minutes?

Arghh. She scanned the room, searching for distraction. Her eyes landed on a chess set. A beautiful hand-carved chess set.

At her indrawn breath, audible in the silence of the room, Kent spun to face her. 'What?' He glanced around as if searching for a spider or lizard, some creepy-crawly that may have frightened her.

'I…' She pointed. 'Did you make that?'

He grunted and shrugged.

'It's beautiful.' She stared at him, trying to recognise the creator of the work of art in the hard stern man in front of her. 'It's one of the most beautiful things I've ever seen.'

'Then you need to get out more.'

She'd have laughed at his response if she hadn't been so engrossed in admiring the individual chess pieces. Each one was intricately carved into the shape of a tree. The skill and workmanship that had gone into each piece took her breath away. The kings were mighty oaks, the queens graceful weeping willows and the bishops upright poplars. Talk about a craft project!

She held her breath and reached out to pick up a pawn— a miniature banksia—and marvelled at the detail. She could see each cylindrical flower on the delicate branches. How on earth had he managed that?

'Do you play?'

She jumped, startled by his closeness. His breath disturbed the hair at her temple as he leant over to survey the piece she held. 'I…'

He took a step back and she found she could breathe again.

'Not really.' She placed the pawn back on the board and sadness pierced her. She tried to smile. 'My father was teaching me before he fell ill.'

The rest of Kent Black could look as hard as stone, but his eyes could soften from a winter gale to a spring breeze in the time it took to draw breath. Josie's heart started to pound.

'I'm sorry about your father, Josie.'

'Thank you.' *He'd called her Josie.*

'I'm sorry he never had a chance to finish teaching you how to play.'

'Me too.' She couldn't look away.

'I'll give you lessons if you like.'

She wondered if she looked as surprised by the offer as he did. She had no intention of letting him off the hook, though. 'I'd like that very much.'

He grunted and took a step back. With one blink his eyes became as carved-from-rock hard as the rest of him.

'When?' she persisted. 'Now?'

'No.' He strode back to the table. 'Monday afternoons,' he said after a pause. 'At about this time.'

It was Tuesday now. Monday was six whole days away. He'd done that on purpose, she was sure of it. She'd missed out one lesson already if you counted yesterday.

She wanted to stamp a foot in frustration. The glint in his eye told her he knew it too. She forced her lips into a smile instead. 'I'll look forward to it.' Beggars couldn't be choosers, and she now only had six afternoons a week to fill. She didn't want him retracting the offer.

She wondered if she could talk him into two afternoons a week? One look at his face told her to leave it for now.

'Why don't we have our tea outside?' He lifted a tray holding their tea things and Josie had no choice but to follow him back out into the sunshine.

She cut large wedges of cake whilst he poured out mugs of tea. He made no attempt at conversation and, strangely, Josie didn't mind. She watched him instead. He devoured his slice of chocolate cake with the kind of hunger that did strange things to her insides.

Warm, fuzzy things.

She had to glance away when he licked the frosting from his fingers. She cut him another slice then cleared her throat. 'Did you grow up around here?'

'No.'

He physically drew back in his seat, his face shuttered,

and disappointment filtered through her. He didn't want her prying into his background. Though at least she now knew his unique brand of strength wasn't something born and bred into him because he'd grown up out here on Eagle Reach. There was hope for her yet.

He eyed her warily. She smiled back. 'It's only a packet mix.' She motioned to the cake. 'I make a much better one from scratch.'

'It's good.'

His manners were improving, but the wariness didn't leave his eyes. It made her feel…wrong. She couldn't remember making anyone feel wary before. She didn't like the sensation. She searched for something deliberately inconsequential to say. She stared at the cake. Her lips twitched. 'I was sorry I didn't pack hundreds and thousands to sprinkle on top.'

Kent choked.

'But then I figured you probably weren't a hundreds and thousands kind of guy. A chocolate-sprinkle kind of guy maybe, but not hundreds and thousands.'

Kent stared at her. Then his wariness fled. He threw his head back and laughed. It changed him utterly, and it stole Josie's breath.

One thing became brilliantly and dazzlingly clear. She could certainly imagine this incarnation of Kent kissing a woman. She saw it in bright Technicolor vividness.

Seeing it, though, didn't mean she wanted it.

It didn't.

Kent rolled his shoulders, stretching out the aches in his muscles. He'd spent most of the day fixing a broken fence and he was dying for his afternoon cup of tea.

And the rest of that chocolate cake Josie had baked yesterday. He couldn't remember the last time he'd eaten anything quite so satisfying. His stomach grumbled low and long. His mouth watered. He reached out to unlatch the back gate then froze.

'Kent?'

Josie.

He peered over the palings and found her standing on the top step of his house, hand raised to knock on his back door. In her other hand she held a plate of what looked suspiciously like freshly baked biscuits.

His stomach growled again. His mouth watered some more. In the sunlight her hair glowed all the hues of a varnished piece of sandalwood and his stomach clenched. He couldn't believe he'd ever thought it mousy. Anticipation leapt to life in his chest. He reached out to unlatch the gate again when reality crashed around him.

This couldn't happen. He didn't do afternoon tea parties.

You don't do chess lessons either, a wry voice in his head pointed out.

Yeah, well, as soon as he found a way to get out of those you could bet your life he would.

'Kent?'

Her soft contralto voice tugged at him. She turned to survey the surrounding area and with a muffled oath he ducked down behind the fence.

Grown men don't hide behind fences, he told himself. For Pete's sake, what would it hurt to have another cup of tea with her? Yesterday's hadn't killed him.

A scowl shuffled through him. He knew exactly how it would hurt. He'd recognised the loneliness in her eyes. If he had a cup of tea again with her today it'd become a habit. A daily thing. She'd start to rely on him. He scowled down at his work-roughened hands. He wasn't going to let that happen.

He'd seen the flash of awareness in her eyes yesterday. He knew exactly where that would lead, because in the space of a heartbeat desire had thrummed through him in unequivocal response. He'd be an idiot to ignore it.

If he met with Josie Peterson for afternoon tea today, she'd be in his bed by the end of the week.

His skin went hard and tight at the thought.

But he knew women like Josie didn't indulge in affairs.

And men like him didn't offer anything more.

He edged away from the fence and stole back the way he'd come, throbbing with a mixture of guilt and desire. He tried to tell himself this was best for both of them. Somehow, though, the sentiment rang hollow.

A spurt of anger shot through him, lending speed to his feet. Darn her for invading his space. Darn her for invading his refuge.

CHAPTER FOUR

JOSIE woke on Thursday morning to rain. She sat on her tiny veranda in the gaily patterned camp chair she'd bought on her trip into Gloucester yesterday, her hands curled around her morning coffee, and stared out into the greyness. Given half a chance she feared that greyness would invade her.

She dropped a hand to Molly's head. 'It doesn't look like we'll get a walk in today.' That had been the plan—a big hike. Especially since Kent had assured her goannas weren't ferocious carnivores.

The rain put paid to that.

She wondered if the rain affected Kent's work. She wondered if he'd be home if she knocked at his back door with muffins this afternoon.

Was he even OK? She hadn't clapped eyes on him since Tuesday afternoon. What if he'd fallen in some gully and broken his leg? What if a brown snake had bitten him? What if—?

Stop it! He'd lived at Eagle Reach for heaven only knew how many years. He wasn't going to start breaking legs or getting bitten by snakes because she'd shown up. Besides,

Molly would know if something was wrong. Josie glanced down at the dog and bit her lip. She would, wouldn't she?

Face it. Kent just didn't need people the way she did. Yesterday she'd sat in two different cafés in Gloucester's main street, lapping up the noise and bustle along with her coffee. In a few days, when the isolation became too much, she'd do it again.

Not today, though. Today she'd start one of her craft projects—the embroidered cushion, or the latch-hook wall hanging, or the candle-making. Or she could finish reading the newspapers. She'd seized every available paper yesterday and wasn't halfway through them yet. Or she could start reading one of the novels she'd bought. She'd bought six.

She drained her coffee and strode inside, determined to make a decision, but the drab bleakness of the cabin's interior sucked all the energy out of her. It really was horrible. Ugly.

Yesterday, when she hadn't found Kent home, she'd come back here, collapsed into a chair and stared at a wall until the dark had gathered about her and she couldn't see her surroundings any more.

It had frightened her when she finally came back to herself. She didn't want that happening again.

'You know what, Molly?' Molly's tail thumped against the bare floorboards in instant response. 'If I want to stay sane for the next month we're going to have to spend today making this place fit to live in.'

She threw open her suitcase and rifled through its contents, searching for inspiration. Suddenly, she laughed. Sarongs! She'd packed her sarongs.

That was when she'd imagined cabins to mean pretty little cabanas set in lush gardens, encircling a lagoon-style swimming pool. Back when she'd pictured banana loungers and exotic drinks in coconut shells with colour-ful paper umbrellas sticking out of them at jaunty angles.

She'd pictured comfort and ease. Relaxation. Not bare, lonely landscapes that stretched as wide as the empty places inside her.

She pulled the sarongs out in a hasty rush then switched on her brand-new transistor radio. She tuned it to one of those ubiquitous radio stations that played cheerful, inane pop, twenty-four-seven. She'd push back the greyness. Somehow. And cheerful and inane would do very nicely at the moment, thank you.

'OK.' Josie pulled in a breath. 'Are you ready for the big test?'

Molly wagged her tail.

Josie drank the last of her tea, crossed her fingers and leapt to her feet. She'd worked on the interior of the cabin for hours. Now came the test—to walk through the door and see if it still sucked the lifeblood from her.

Without giving herself any more time to think, Josie strode across the threshold and into the cabin. She held her breath and completed a slow circle. With a sigh of relief, almost a sob, she dropped to her knees and hugged Molly hard. 'Now this is a place I can live in for the next month. What do you say?'

Molly's answer was a wet lick up the side of her face. Laughing, Josie jumped up. OK, what to do for the rest of the day?

Her eyes fell on the notepad on the table. The what-am-I-going-to-do-with-the-rest-of-my-life-and-what-skills-do-I-have? notepad. Her heart dropped, her shoulders sagged. She gulped back a hard ball of panic.

'Muffins.' Her voice held a high edge that stopped

Molly's tail mid-wag. 'Which would your master prefer, do you think? Date and walnut or apple and cinnamon?'

Kent swore when the knock sounded on his back door. He set down the chess piece he was carving and glanced at his watch. Two o'clock.

Four o'clock on Tuesday. Three o'clock yesterday. She wouldn't last the week at this rate.

Good. He clenched his jaw. Josie Peterson was getting as pesky as a darn mosquito. And as persistent. He rubbed the back of his neck. He could always sneak out the front way. She'd never know.

No. She wasn't chasing him out of his house. Another knock sounded. He gritted his teeth. She wasn't worming her way into it either. The sooner he set the ground rules the easier the next month would be. He stormed to the back door and flung it open. As he expected, Josie stood there. The rain had stopped, the sun hadn't come out, but her hair still gleamed like burnished sandalwood, which for some reason irritated him.

'What?' he barked. No pretence at friendliness, no pretence at politeness.

Josie's face fell. He hardened his heart and hated himself for it.

'I, umm…' She moistened her lips. 'I've been baking and I've made too much for one. It seems a shame to waste it all, though. I thought you might like some.'

The aroma of freshly baked muffins mingled with her fresh, fruity fragrance and ploughed straight into his gut. He couldn't remember the last time he'd faced so much temptation. 'You thought wrong,' he snapped.

Strong. He had to stay strong.

Darn it! Those muffins looked good. Dangerously good. Just like her. He had a feeling he could get used to her cooking. If the truth be told, he had a feeling he could get used to her, and that couldn't happen. He'd let her down. The way he'd let—

The gold flecks in her eyes suddenly flashed. 'You didn't mind the chocolate cake the other day.' Her chin quivered when she stuck it out. 'We had a very pleasant half an hour over that cake.'

Precisely. Which was why it wasn't going to happen again. 'Look, Ms Peterson—'

'Josie.'

'I am not your nursemaid. I am not your friend. I am the man you've rented a cabin from for a month and that's as far as our association goes, got it?'

Her eyes widened at his bluntness. Her mouth worked. 'Don't you get lonely?' she finally blurted out.

'Nope.' Not any more. Not most of the time anyway.

'So how do you do it?' She lifted the plate of muffins as if they could provide an answer. 'How do you manage to live out here all on your own and not mind?'

He could see it wasn't idle curiosity. She wanted to know. Needed to know, maybe. He supposed he'd started off much the same way she was now.

Not the searching out of human contact. He'd shunned that from the start. But he'd carved and whittled wood the way she baked. He'd kept himself busy with cattle and cabins and carving until the days had taken on a shape of their own.

So he didn't need the likes of her coming around here now and disrupting it. Making him ache for things that couldn't be.

She shook her head. 'You can't be human.'

He wished that were true.

'We all need people.'

'Believe me, some needy fly-by-night is not essential to my well-being.'

She paled at his words and he loathed himself all the more. His resolve started to waver and weaken. 'What do you see happening between us?' he snapped out. 'You'll be gone in a month.' Probably less. That thought steeled his determination again.

'Friends?' she whispered.

He laughed, a harsh sound that scraped out of his throat leaving it raw. He had to get rid of her. She could capture a man with those sad, gold-flecked eyes and the soft curve of her lips. It'd all end in tears. Her tears. Then he'd really hate himself.

She took one step back, then another, her face white. 'You are a piece of work, you know that?'

Yep. It wasn't news to him. But Josie wasn't cut out for all this. 'Try the general store in Martin's Gully.' He nodded at the plate in her hand. 'They might be interested in placing an order or two with you.'

Liz Perkins would take Josie under her ample, matronly wing. It'd do both of them the world of good. On that thought, he slammed the door in Josie's face before guilt got the better of him and he hauled her inside and tried to make amends.

Josie stalked back to her cabin, quivering all over with outrage. She ranted in incoherent half-sentences to Molly.

'Of all the arrogant assumptions! Needy fly-by-night? Who does he think he is?'

She slammed the plate to the kitchen bench and paced. Ha! At least she'd eradicated his grey presence from her cabin. Satisfaction shot through her when she surveyed the changes she'd made.

'And he needn't think I'm going to sit around here all afternoon and moon about it either.'

Molly whined and pushed her nose against Josie's hand. Josie dropped to her knees and scratched Molly's ears. 'I'm sorry, girl. It's not your fault. You're lovely and loyal and sweet and too good for the likes of him. It's not your fault you drew the short straw when it came to masters.'

Molly rolled onto her back and groaned with pleasure when Josie scratched her tummy. 'You're gorgeous and beautiful.'

Her fingers brushed the scar that zigzagged across Molly's abdomen and she stilled. 'I don't get him at all.' She meant to take his advice, though.

It took exactly twelve and a half minutes to reach the tiny township of Martin's Gully. It wasn't exactly a blink-and-miss town, but it wasn't far from it. It had, at the most, two-dozen houses, though it boasted its own tiny wooden church. Completing the picture was a post office that, according to the sign in its window, opened two and a half days a week, and Perkins' General Store.

Josie pushed through the door of the latter then waited for her eyes to adjust to the dimness. She blinked as the size of the interior came into focus. Bags of feed grain competed with tools for floor space on her left. Bolts of material lined the wall. On her right, shelves full of tinned food and every known grocery item arced away from her. Down the middle sat an old-fashioned freezer. The store smelt dry and dusty and good.

'Can I help you?' a thin, middle-aged woman hailed her from behind the counter at the rear of the room.

Someone with a smile. Josie hastened towards her. 'Hi, I'm Josie Peterson. I'm staying at Eagle Reach for the next few weeks.'

'Bridget Anderson.' Her eyes narrowed as she shook Josie's proffered hand. 'Ain't Eagle Reach Kent Black's place?'

Josie nodded. She'd have thought everyone in Martin's Gully would know everybody else's business. Maybe Kent Black maintained an unfriendly distance with the folk in town too?

As if reading her mind, the other woman leaned in closer. 'This is my sister's store. I'm helping out for a bit.'

Another newcomer? Fellow feeling rushed through Josie.

'Lizzie's husband, Ted, died back in November.'

'Oh, that's awful.'

'And she won't have a word said against Kent Black.'

Really? Josie tried to stop her eyebrows from shooting straight up into her hairline. So, Kent had at least one friend in town, did he?

Bridget's face darkened. 'Me, on the other hand…'

'He's very solitary,' Josie offered, she hoped tactfully.

Bridget snorted. 'Downright unfriendly if you ask me.'

She recalled Kent's black glare. Ooh, yes, she'd agree. Not that she had any intention of saying so, of course.

'Though a body can understand it, what with all that tragedy in his past and all.'

'Tragedy?' The word slipped out before she could help it.

'Aye. His father tried to murder the entire family in their beds as they slept. Set fire to the house in the wee hours of the morning. Kent was the only one that got out. It claimed his mother and sister, his father too.'

Josie's jaw dropped. The room spun. She gripped the

counter top for support. 'That's…that's one of the most awful things I've ever heard.'

'Aye. The father was a violent man, from all accounts.'

What accounts?

'You wanna hear the worst of it?'

No, she didn't. She'd heard enough. But she couldn't move to shake her head. She'd frozen to a block of ice.

'Kent had taken the mother and sister to live with him, to protect them. Didn't work out, though, did it?'

Bile rose in Josie's throat. No wonder Kent scowled and growled and hid away as he did. To lose his entire family in such an awful way.

She promptly forgave him every unfriendly scowl, each clipped word and all the times he'd turned away without so much as a backward glance. But was burying yourself away from the entire human race the answer? She remembered the way he'd tucked into her chocolate cake. She bet he was hungry for a whole lot more than flour and sugar.

Bridget opened her mouth to add what Josie imagined would be more lurid details, so she quickly peeled the lid off her container and held it out, hastily changing the subject. 'I was wondering if there'd be a market for any home-baked goodies around here at all?'

Bridget's nose quivered appreciatively. She reached in, seized a muffin and greedily devoured it. 'Mmm… We can see how they go, love.' She brushed crumbs off her fingers. 'You never know what'll happen once word gets around.' Her eyes narrowed. 'But if you're only here on holiday, what you doing cookin'?'

Josie gulped. She didn't want to be the latest object of Bridget's gossip. 'It's a hobby,' she lied. 'I wanted to try out some new recipes while I had the time, that's all.'

Bridget helped herself to another muffin. 'What are your other specialities?'

'What do you think would sell well?'

'Caramel slice, homemade shortbread, lemon meringue pie.'

She wondered if Bridget was merely reciting her own list of favourites.

'The church fête is on Sunday. We're always looking for goodies to sell. Why don't you make up a few batches of whatever you like and see how they go over?'

If Josie had ears like Molly they'd have immediately pricked forward. A church fête? This Sunday? That gave her something to do over the weekend. Time suddenly didn't hang quite so heavily about her. 'That sounds like fun.'

'Lizzie and me, we're manning our own stall. Would you like to join us, love?'

Would she what? 'It sounds lovely.'

'Have you ever made a Mars-bar slice? Give it a go,' she advised when Josie shook her head. 'It'll be a real winner.'

Josie's lips twitched as Bridget reached for a third muffin. From where she was standing, the feedback was already pretty positive. At this rate there wouldn't be any muffins left for the rest of Martin's Gully to sample.

That was OK. She'd bake more for Sunday.

But as she drove back to Eagle's Reach it wasn't church fêtes or muffin and slice recipes that wove through her mind, but the awful history Bridget had related about Kent. More than anything, she found herself wishing she could do something for him. Something more than chocolate cake.

CHAPTER FIVE

FRIDAY morning Josie drove into Gloucester, stocked up on supplies and bought a recipe book.

Friday afternoon she and Molly went for a big walk. Kent was right. The trails leading down to the river really were very pretty. Not that she had a chance to tell him. She didn't clap eyes on him.

Friday night she made toffee and rum balls.

Saturday morning she made muffins, caramel slice, a Mars-bar slice and cooked chocolate cake from scratch.

Saturday afternoon she found a tick at her waist.

She promptly sat, took a deep breath and tried to remember her first aid. She was an AIN, for heaven's sake, an Assistant in Nursing. She gulped, but her mind went blank. Her kind of nursing hadn't involved ticks. It had involved watching her father die.

She peeled back the waistband of her shorts and stared at the tick again. She must've picked it up on her walk yesterday. It wriggled. Ugh. She hastily folded the waistband back into place. What if there were more? What if she was covered in ticks?

The entire surface of her skin started to itch.

'Don't be ridiculous,' she said out loud. But panic and

adrenaline surged through her. Did adrenaline do anything to ticks? She gulped. It probably turned them into super-ticks or something.

'Oh, get a grip.'

Molly whined and rested her head on Josie's lap. Josie stared down at the trusting brown eyes and stiffened. What if Molly had ticks too? How did you get ticks off a dog? She surged to her feet. She'd have to ask Kent.

Josie was proud of herself for not racing as fast as she could for Kent's back door and pounding on it with both fists. She made herself walk at an even pace, a quick even pace, and when she reached his door she raised her hand and knocked twice. A quick rat-tat.

His frown was the first thing she registered. She raised her hand before he could say something sharp and cutting. 'I just want to ask a quick question, that's all. It won't take long, I swear.'

'Well?' he snapped when she paused.

'What…what is the treatment for ticks?'

Kent stared at her for a moment. The dark blue eyes did strange things to her insides as they roamed across her face. With a smothered oath, he seized her elbow and pulled her inside.

'Where?' he demanded, letting her go and planting his hands on his hips.

'Please check Molly first. She's smaller than me and I hear ticks can do nasty things to dogs.' Awful, terrible things like paralysis and…and worse.

'They can do nasty things to humans too.'

When Josie folded her hands flat against her stomach and said nothing, he raised his eyes to the ceiling. 'Molly will be fine. I give her a monthly tablet.'

Josie sagged. Relief pounded through her. 'Thank heavens. I'd thought…' The rest of her words dried up in her throat as Kent continued to stare at her.

'Where is this tick?'

She had a sudden vision of his strong, tanned fingers on her flesh and her pulse started to pound. 'If you, umm, just tell me what I should do I'll take care of it. I don't mean to put you out or anything.'

She didn't think she wanted Kent touching her. She had a feeling it'd be a whole lot safer for her peace of mind if he didn't. His lips twitched as if he knew exactly what she was thinking, and Josie's heart hammered all the way into her throat and back again.

'What you need to do, Josie, is point to the tick.'

Her name rolled off his tongue, thick and sweet like golden syrup. It turned her insides thick and syrupy too.

The twitch of his lips became a kind of half-grin. 'Trust me.' He waggled his fingers. 'I'm a doctor.'

'Yeah, right.' The one thing she did trust was that he wholly enjoyed her discomfort. She remembered what Bridget had said the day before yesterday and surrendered with a sigh. 'Here.' She peeled back the waistband of her shorts to show him.

He crouched down beside her, his fingers gentle on her skin as he turned her towards the light. Then he leapt up, grabbed a jar of Vaseline from beneath the sink, crouched down beside her again and swiped a generous glob of the ointment across the tick's body.

'Vaseline?' Her voice was breathy. She wondered if he felt the leap of her blood against his fingertips. Oh, boy. She'd known there were areas of her life she'd neglected in the last few months, but this was ridiculous.

'Ticks breathe through their rear-ends. It can't breathe through the Vaseline, so it'll work its way out. Then I'll pick it off with these.' He held up a pair of tweezers. 'It means there's little chance of the head breaking off.'

She gulped. 'Good.' She didn't want the tick leaving any of its body parts behind, thank you. She didn't want to know what would happen if it did either.

'Do you have any more?'

His words cut through a fog that seemed to have descended around her brain. 'More ticks?'

His lips twitched again. 'Yes.'

'Oh, umm.' She shrugged. 'I don't know.'

'Spin for me.'

She did. His finger trailed across the bare flesh of her waist as she turned, making her suck in a breath.

'All clear there, now sit.' He pushed her into a kitchen chair. 'Ticks, like most other living creatures, choose warm, protected places to live.'

'Uh-huh.' It was about as much as she could manage.

'Like behind the ears and at the nape of the neck.'

He brushed her hair to one side and it was all she could do not to melt against him as his fingers moved across said areas. Up this close his heat buffeted her. As did his hot man scent, a combination of wood and wood smoke and freshly cut grass. She wanted to breathe him in and never stop.

Crazy thought. Nerves skittered through her. 'Thank you for the tip about taking my muffins into the general store.' She knew she was about to start babbling, but she needed to distract herself somehow and babbling seemed relatively innocuous, given the alternatives racing through her mind.

'Did you meet Liz Perkins?'

She seized the question as a verbal lifeline and tried for all she was worth to erect some kind of metaphorical wall between them. 'Umm, no.'

The metaphorical-wall thing wasn't working. It did nothing to assuage the sensations that pounded through her when he swept her hair across the other side of her neck. She closed her eyes and bit back a groan.

'Liz wasn't there.' Concentrate, she ordered herself. 'I met her sister, Bridget.'

Kent's humph told her exactly what he thought of Bridget.

She didn't blame him. Not when she recalled how eager Bridget had been to impart her information. Guilt squirmed through her. She'd listened, hadn't she?

'I'm going to the church fête on Sunday,' she rushed on quickly. 'Tomorrow.' Sunday was tomorrow, she reminded herself. Though, with Kent standing this close, she wouldn't swear to it. She wouldn't swear which way was up.

His fingers stilled. 'Is that why you're cooking up a storm?'

'Uh-huh.' How'd he know she was cooking up a storm?

'The smells have been wafting up the hill,' he said as if she'd asked the question out loud. His fingers moved across her neck again. 'It smells good.'

'What's your favourite sweet treat?' If he told her she'd make it for him. As a thank-you, nothing more. She certainly wouldn't make the mistake of expecting him to share it or anything.

'Why?'

She winced at the sudden harsh note in his voice. 'No reason, just looking for inspiration,' she lied. 'Bridget asked me to make a Mars-bar slice.'

He finished checking her neck and she breathed a sigh of relief when he moved away, but only for a moment, as he almost immediately crouched down beside her to check the tick at her waist again.

'It needs a couple more minutes.'

He moved off abruptly to a chair opposite, and, contrarily, Josie missed the warmth of his hands, the touch of his breath against her flesh.

His eyes narrowed on her face. 'You feel OK? Any nausea or wooziness?'

'No.' Unbalanced by his touch, maybe, but she had a feeling that was not what he meant.

'So, Bridget has roped you into all that baking?'

'No.' She lifted her chin. Not everyone found her company abhorrent. 'She and Liz are manning a stall and I'm going to help.'

He gave a short laugh. 'She's an opportunist, that one. I'll give her that.'

'I wanted to do it.' But then she recalled how Bridget had said more muffins would go down a treat, not to mention a chocolate cake. And that if Josie had time, maybe she could come by early and help them set up the trestle table for the stall too.

She shook her head impatiently. It didn't matter. She wanted to help. It'd be fun. The knowing twist of his lips, though, irked her. 'Are you going?'

'Me? You're joking, right?'

'Why not?' She lifted her hands. 'This is a tiny community. You should support it.'

'By letting the Bridgets of the town get their claws into me? No, thank you very much. I've far better things to do on a Sunday than be hounded into helping set up stalls and manning the chocolate wheel.'

Like what? she wanted to ask. She didn't, though. She

didn't dare. 'I think it'll be fun. It's not like you'd have to do anything. Just…'

'Just what?' he mocked.

'Just take part,' she snapped back.

Then wished she hadn't as everything she'd found out about Kent yesterday rose up inside her. Her stomach burned acid. 'You're right. Bridget is a terrible gossip. But it doesn't necessarily follow that she's a bad person. And not everyone in Martin's Gully is like that, surely?'

His eyes darkened and narrowed in on her in the space of a heartbeat.

Josie flushed and twisted her hands together. She knew precisely how guilty she looked. 'Bridget told me what happened to your mother and sister,' she blurted out.

Kent reared back as if her words had slapped him. His face paled. Dark red slashed his cheekbones. 'She had no right—'

'No, she didn't,' Josie hastily agreed. 'No right at all.' She wanted to reach out and touch him, but was too afraid to. 'I'm sorry. What happened to them…' She lifted her hands again. 'It must've been the most awful thing in the world.' His eyes glittered dangerously. 'I'm sorry,' she repeated. She wanted to say so much more but didn't have the words for it.

He stared at her as if he didn't know what to say. She didn't know what to say either.

His gaze dropped to her waist. 'That tick should be ready to come out now.'

Before she was aware of it, he'd tweezered it out.

'Thank you.' Her breath hitched at his nearness. She rose and took a hasty step back. 'Would you like me to bring you anything from the fête?'

'Like?'

'I don't know.' She had an awful feeling she was babbling again. 'Maybe you have a secret yearning for Mrs Elwood's tomato chutney or Mr Smith's home-produced honey?'

'There aren't any Mrs Elwoods in Martin's Gully.'

'Any Mr Smiths?'

'Several, but none of them are beekeepers.'

She edged towards his back door. 'So, no tomato chutney or honey, then?'

'No, thank you.'

'OK.' She practically fell down the back steps. 'Goodnight, then.'

'Josie.'

She turned back, her heart thumping.

'I…'

She held her breath, but she hardly knew what she was waiting for.

'You need to shower. You need to check under your arms and behind your knees. Anywhere a tick might get.'

'OK.' She waited but when he didn't add anything else she gave a tiny wave then fled.

Josie left early the next morning. Kent knew because he watched. His lips drew back from his teeth in a grimace. So Bridget Anderson had roped Josie into setting up the stall, huh?

He remembered the way Josie had hugged Molly that first day. He remembered the feel of her curves pressed against him as she'd slid out of that tree and down his body. He shook his head and called himself every kind of idiot he could think of. Josie Peterson could look after herself. She wasn't his responsibility.

'Go check the cattle,' he growled out loud. At least they were something he was responsible for.

Not that checking the cattle required much effort. More a case of checking the levels in the water troughs, checking the fences, making sure the steers hadn't picked up an injury or were showing signs of disease.

Checking the cattle took less than an hour.

He wondered how Josie was finding the fête. He bet her goodies sold fast. He bet Bridget Anderson had her stuck behind that stall all day. He bet she wouldn't even get a chance to buy a ticket in the chocolate wheel.

Josie would like the chocolate wheel.

For Pete's sake! 'Go clean the cabins.'

He grabbed the bucket of cleaning supplies and an ancient wooden broom. He averted his gaze as he stalked past Josie's cabin. His nostrils flared, though, and he imagined, if he took a deep enough breath, her fresh, fruity fragrance would fill his lungs.

He held his breath and tried to banish her from his mind.

By lunchtime he'd finished cleaning the cabins. Every surface gleamed with fresh-scrubbed cleanliness. Just as they had before he'd started.

He averted his gaze as he stalked past her cabin again, but he remembered the way her eyes had filled with a soft light when she'd told him how sorry she was about his mother and sister. He couldn't doubt her sincerity. He'd wanted to rage and stamp and throw things, but that soft light in her eyes had held him still.

Nobody in Martin's Gully, not even Liz Perkins, had dared mention his past. He hadn't encouraged them to. He hadn't confided in a single soul. But they all knew what had happened and they skirted around the subject, skirted around him. Not Josie, though. He couldn't help but admire her honesty, her guts.

Her generosity.

A generosity he didn't doubt Bridget Anderson was taking advantage of right now.

He stowed away the broom and bucket then glanced around the kitchen. Darn it! He jammed his hat on his head and grabbed his car keys. He had a sudden craving for tomato chutney and honey. He refused to acknowledge any more than that.

Kent spotted Josie straight away, sitting all by herself at the far end of a row of trestle tables. Her hair gleamed, but her shoulders sagged. The rest of the town congregated on the opposite side of the field around a flatbed truck for the traditional auction. He bit back an oath, adjusted the brim of his hat and headed towards her.

Her eyes widened when he strode up. 'Kent! What are you doing here? I mean…' She glanced away then back again as if trying to moderate her surprise. 'I didn't think this was your thing.'

'I'm all out of tomato chutney and honey,' he muttered.

She smiled then, and it kicked him right in the gut. With a flourish, she waved her arm across the table. 'Can I tempt you with any of our goodies?'

Our? He recognised Liz's gramma pies and choko pickles, but he'd bet Josie had contributed the rest. 'How long have you been stuck behind there?'

Her smile slipped. 'It doesn't matter. I'm sure once the auction is over Bridget will be back and—'

'You haven't moved from there all morning, have you? You haven't even had a chance to look around yet?'

'There's still plenty of time.'

'Have you had lunch?' he barked.

She started to laugh. 'I'm being punished for skipping breakfast. Smell that,' she ordered. She pulled in a big breath and he practically saw her start to salivate. 'They've set up a sausage sizzle behind the church hall and all I can smell is frying onions. It's pure torture.'

He could tell she was only joking, but a surge of anger shot through him. Bloody Bridget. 'Where's Liz?'

'Sick.'

Sick of her sister, he'd bet.

Josie's skin was pale and he could see it starting to turn pink in the sun. She'd erected a canopy to shelter the food, but not one for herself.

'C'mon.' He waved a hand, practically ordering her out from behind the trestle table.

'I can't leave.'

'Why not? Everyone else has.'

'But...but I told Bridget I'd man the fort and...then there's the money tin and—'

'Give it to me.'

'But...'

He reached over and took it, placing it firmly in the middle of the table. 'Now seems to me you've done your share. If Bridget wants the stall manned, she'll come back when she sees it's empty. Right then, see that weeping willow down by the river?' He pointed and she nodded. 'Grab us something,' he nodded at the table, 'and meet me down there.'

'I can't just take something.'

'Why not? You cooked it.'

She drew herself up. 'It's for charity!'

He laughed at the outrage plastered across her face.

Josie Peterson made him feel light years younger. He fished out a twenty-dollar note from his pocket, held it out for her to see then put it into the money tin.

Her jaw dropped. 'That's too much.'

'It's for charity, isn't it?'

She stared then laughed, and it throbbed through him in all the places he shouldn't be thinking about.

'So, you're pretty hungry, huh?'

'Starved.' And it'd take a whole lot more than sugar to satisfy his cravings.

'The weeping willow?'

'The weeping willow,' he agreed.

With that he turned and headed straight across the field before he could pull Josie over the trestle table and kiss her.

When she reached the tree, Josie had to admit Kent had chosen a pretty spot for a picnic. The river slid by, silver and silent, meditative. It soothed the sore, bruised places inside her. She wondered if it did the same for Kent. Maybe that was why he chose to bury himself out here.

Settling on the grass beneath the tree, she welcomed the shade and the almost hypnotic sway of fronds in the breeze, and wondered about her unusual rescue. And her even more unusual rescuer.

Kent, carrying sausage sandwiches and cans of lemonade, appeared and Josie's hunger momentarily overrode her other concerns. 'Mmm.' She closed her eyes and savoured her first bite. 'This is fabulous.' When she opened them again she found Kent staring at her strangely. She suddenly remembered her manners. 'Thank you.'

'You're welcome.'

The faded blue of his chambray shirt highlighted the

brilliant blue of his eyes. The snug fit of his jeans high-lighted the firmness of his thighs. The sudden shortness of Josie's breath highlighted her heretofore unknown par-tiality for firm thigh muscles encased in faded denim.

'I, umm…' She dragged her gaze upwards. 'Thank you for rescuing me…again.' That seemed to be becoming a habit.

'Not a problem.'

Oh, dear. She obviously had a partiality for firm lips and chiselled jaws too. She dragged her gaze to the river and tried to recreate the peace it had invoked in her only moments ago. She ate the rest of her sausage sandwich in silence.

Three ducks, small, brown and dappled, paddled by; bellbirds started up on the other bank. She pulled in a breath and her tension eased out of her, but her awareness for the man opposite didn't.

'When I look at all this,' she motioned to the river, 'I can see why you live out here. It's beautiful.'

'Yep.' A pause. 'You can't imagine living out here yourself?'

'No.' And she couldn't. Too much of it frightened her, even as she admired the starkness of its beauty.

'A city girl at heart?'

She glanced at him sharply, but no scorn or censure marred the perfect blue of his eyes. 'No, not a city girl.' Though she could more easily imagine living in a city than at Eagle Reach. 'I live in a sleepy little town on the coast about three hours north from here.' Her whole frame light-ened when she thought of it. 'It's beautiful. Especially at this time of year.' When summer merged into autumn, the days still warm but the nights cool.

'If it's so pretty there, what are you doing here?'

Good question. Sadness and a thread of something

harsher—anger?—trickled through her. She quashed it. 'My father died. He'd suffered from dementia for a few years. I was his full-time carer. I needed to get away for a bit.'

But somewhere nice. Somewhere she could close her eyes and breathe more freely. Not somewhere that scared her half out of her wits in one instant then stole her breath with its beauty the next. And she hadn't wanted to be shipped off for a whole month. A week would've done.

She gulped. She was an ungrateful wretch.

Kent reached out and covered her hand with his. 'That must've been hard.'

She nodded, her throat thickening with unshed tears at the kindness reflected in the deep blue of his eyes. She could see he understood her grief.

Dear heavens above, of course he did!

She gazed back out at the river, determined not to cry, but as the warmth of his hand stole through her her heart started to pound. She glanced up at him and her mouth went dry. Did he feel it too?

As if in answer, his hand tightened over hers. Exhilaration sped through her when his eyes narrowed on her lips, then desire—hot and hard and relentless. Three feet separated them and she wanted that gap closed, fast. Needed it. She couldn't remember craving a man's touch so intently. She wanted to lose herself in him and not come up for air.

Gripped by forces greater than common sense, Josie swayed towards him, lips parted. Time freeze-framed and lost all meaning, except in the way it sharpened all her senses. Every single muscle ached to meld itself against him. Her fingers, her palm, hungered to caress the dark shading at his jaw. She wanted to breathe in his hot male scent, she wanted to wrap her arms around his neck and slide her fingers through the crisp darkness of his hair.

Hunger flared in his eyes. Her own blood quickened in response. Then, with a tiny shake of his head, he removed his hand and sat back, his mouth a grim line as he stared out at the river. Disappointment flooded her, filling her mouth with the acrid taste of its bitterness.

Embarrassment quickly followed. 'I, umm... Dessert?'

She seized the bag of goodies like a lifeline. 'I didn't know what you felt like so I grabbed a couple of pieces of caramel slice, half a dozen oatmeal biscuits and a slice each of lemon meringue pie and chocolate cake.'

As she named each item she pulled the appropriate paper plate out of the bag and lined them up between them. His twenty dollars deserved a whole lot more than this, but she couldn't have carried anything else. 'I mean, you could've had carrot cake or muffins,' she babbled on, scrunching the plastic carrier bag into a tiny ball and squeezing it. 'But if you'd prefer something else then I'm sure...'

He reached across and halted her movements. The rest of her words dried up in her throat. Her stupid pulse fluttered in her throat.

'It wouldn't have been a good idea.'

She knew he wasn't talking about cake. He was talking about kissing her. She nodded, her throat tight. 'I know.'

He drew back. 'What do you want?' He motioned to the plates.

She seized the oatmeal biscuits, more for something to do, than because she was hungry. Her hunger had fled.

Her hunger for food, that was.

Stop thinking about it!

She flung a glance over her shoulder, searching for

something, anything, and her jaw dropped at the size of the crowd milling in the field behind her. 'Where did they all come from?'

Kent glanced up then shrugged and stretched out on his side. 'I'd heard the fête took off in the afternoon. The folk of Gloucester have caught wind of it in the last few years.'

She glanced at him and tried not to notice how the lean angles of his body stretched out like an invitation. 'Why?'

'A couple of the local specialities have started making names for themselves,' he said, peeling plastic wrap from around the chocolate cake.

Her ears pricked up. 'Like?' She shuffled around on her knees to watch the crowd. Lots of people, lots of laughter— it loosened the knots inside her.

'You mean besides tomato chutney and honey?'

She glanced at him then laughed. So, scowling-don't-get-too-close-to-me Kent could crack a joke…and grin while he did it. She could grow to like this Kent. A lot. 'So, I was on the money with my guess, huh?'

'If you substitute the chutney for Liz's choko pickles then yes.'

His smile crinkled the lines around his eyes. Her stomach flip-flopped.

'They're famous and with some cause. Nothing beats a silverside and choko pickle sandwich.'

She filed that for future reference.

'Except maybe this!' His eyes bugged as he chewed chocolate cake. 'Jeez, Josie.' He stared at her, half in admiration, half in consternation. 'This is…'

'Good?'

'Better than good.'

'I told you I made a better one from scratch.'

He chuckled at the smug toss of her head and her stomach flip-flopped more.

'What else should I be on the look-out for?'

'Chloe Isaac's homemade soap. Popular opinion is divided between the granulated strawberry bar and the smooth lemon myrtle.'

'Ooh, yum. I'm getting both.' She pointed an accusing finger at him, but kept her eyes on the crowd. 'That's the sort of thing you should put in the cabins. People would love it.' She sent him a sly glance. 'What about the honey? Famous too?'

He polished off the rest of the cake with a grin. 'I'll introduce you to our local beekeeper, old Fraser Todd. He'll sell you a pot of honey fresh from the hive with a piece of the honeycomb still in it. You'll never taste anything like it,' he promised.

Her mouth watered. She pushed the plate of biscuits towards him. She'd better save her appetite.

'You think I need fattening up or something?'

'You were the one who said you were hungry. You've still a slice of lemon meringue pie and a couple of pieces of caramel slice to go yet.'

'I'll save them for later.' He nodded towards the stalls with their crowds clustered around them. 'Besides, I'd have thought you'd be eager to get us out amongst them, fighting for all the goodies before they're gone.'

She loved the way he said 'us'; it meant he intended to hang around for a bit. Her blood did a funny little dance through her veins, which she tried to ignore. She lifted a hand that encompassed the scene before her. 'I'm enjoying all this first.'

'Enjoying what?'

'Watching the people having fun, hearing them laugh. It's what I meant when I told Marty and Frank I wanted a break.'

Kent stilled, mid-munch. Carefully, he chewed and swallowed the rest of his biscuit. 'Don't you want to be a part of it?'

'Eventually.' She didn't take her eyes off the crowd, lapping it all up like a starving dog. 'But I'm happy to savour it all first. Ooh, an artist is setting up.'

'She's one of our best-kept secrets.'

Kent collected up the uneaten goodies and placed them back in the bag, then, with his face gentle, offered Josie his hand. 'C'mon, why don't I show you the cream of the town's offerings?'

Josie was more than happy to place her hand in Kent's tanned, capable one and be pulled to her feet, more than ready to become one with the laughing, happy crowd.

CHAPTER SIX

'YOU should be ashamed of yourself,' Josie chided a couple of hours later, collapsing at a picnic table.

'Ashamed of myself?'

What the...? He'd made a sterling effort to play the sociable companion to Josie over the afternoon. What was more, he thought he'd succeeded.

Not that it'd been an effort. No effort at all. It had earned him more than one speculative glance from more than one local, though. Not that he cared. Their gossip couldn't touch him and Josie would be gone in three weeks, so it couldn't hurt her either.

Three weeks. And don't you forget it, he warned himself. He eased his long legs beneath the table to sit opposite her when he had a feeling what he should be doing was getting to his feet and running in the opposite direction.

Fast.

He couldn't. When Josie had made her remarkable declaration about what she really wanted from her holiday— her eyes hungry on the crowd, those peculiarly restful hands of hers folded against her knees and a tendril of weeping willow playing across her shoulder and catching in her hair—he'd gained a sudden insight into all she'd given up when she'd taken on the role of carer to her father.

She didn't need a holiday stuck halfway up a mountain. She needed people, she needed to feel connected again. She needed images of life and laughter to help mitigate the recent images of sickness and death. He understood that. And he cursed her brothers for not seeing it.

He couldn't help that she was stuck halfway up a mountain, but he had taken it upon himself to make sure she enjoyed the fête today. And that no one, including that witch Bridget Anderson, took advantage of her generosity. Now here she was, telling him he should be ashamed of himself? So much for gratitude.

'Why?' he demanded, irked more than he wanted to admit.

She spread her arms wide and he found himself wanting to walk straight into them. He scowled. 'What?'

'Look at the wealth of all this local produce.'

He reckoned she'd bought just about every example of it too. That made him grin. Her delight in the smallest of things had touched him. 'And?'

'With all this available at your fingertips, how could you possibly make such a sorry job on those cabins?'

'Sorry job!' His jaw dropped. He jabbed the air between them with a finger. 'I know Eagle Reach isn't exactly the Ritz, but—'

Her snort cut him short. 'You can say that again.'

'Look, you're not my usual grade of clientele.'

She leaned forward. 'I know you keep saying the cabins attract the tough, rugged outdoor types, but really…' She leaned back, arms outspread again.

He wished she'd stop doing that. 'What?' He lifted a hand. 'What?' The cabins were perfectly…adequate.

'Would it really be such an effort to make them a little more inviting?'

She had to be joking, right?

'Even rough, rugged outdoor types like something nice to come home to after all that hiking and fishing or whatever it is rough, rugged outdoor types do.'

'So…so you want me to put strawberry-scented soap in the bathrooms,' he spluttered, 'and…and frangipani-scented candles in the living rooms?' It'd make him a laughing stock.

'Maybe not the strawberry soap,' she allowed. 'That might not be a big hit with your tough types, but what about the mint and eucalyptus soap, huh? It'd add a bit of local colour and wouldn't threaten anyone's masculinity. What's wrong with that? It's a nice touch.'

She folded her arms and glared at him. He folded his arms and glared back.

'A couple of Mrs Gower's rag rugs wouldn't go astray either.'

Rugs!

'Not to mention a painting or two.'

OK, so the cabins were bare. He'd admit that much.

'And I know you're not a fruit and flowers kind of guy—'

It was his turn to snort. 'You can say that again.'

'But,' she persisted, 'a jar of Mr Todd's honey and Liz's choko pickles would be a friendly gesture. To the town as well as the guests.'

He wished he could ignore the way the gold flecks in her eyes flashed when she got all fired up, or the way her pretty little chin pointed at him, angling her lips in a way that made his mouth water.

Not good. He shouldn't be thinking about kissing her. He clenched his hands beneath the table to stop from reaching out and grabbing that pretty little chin in his fingers and slanting his lips over hers. Heck, that'd get the gossips' tongues wagging.

'You know what?'

'What?' The word growled out of him from between teeth that were likewise clenched. Fortunately, or unfortunately, his gruffness didn't so much as make her blink any more.

'I think you're afraid of making those cabins too home-like.'

He jerked back.

'I think you're afraid to make any place too much like home.'

Something started to thud painfully in his chest. He tried to throw her words off, but found he couldn't. 'All this because I like simple and plain?' he snapped.

Not so much as a blink. 'Either that or you're afraid of making them so nice that you'll have to share your mountain with all of the repeat business you'd get.'

The thudding eased to an ache at her teasing.

'You could be on to something, lass. Our Kent here doesn't like to share his solitude.'

Kent jumped up, pleasure lighting through him at the sight of Clancy Whitehall's dancing dark eyes and thatch of white hair. He helped the elderly man to a seat. 'Clancy, this is Josie Peterson. She's staying at Eagle Reach for a few weeks.'

'A pleasure. Clancy Whitehall.' He introduced himself before Kent had a chance. His dark eyes danced across Josie's face as he shook her hand. 'I have the dubious distinction of being Martin's Gully's oldest resident.'

Josie broke into one of those grins that hit Kent square in the gut. 'Pleased to meet you, Mr Whitehall.'

'Call me Clancy, please. Mr Whitehall was my father.'

Josie laughed, her eyes darting to Kent's to share her delight. Kent could've groaned out loud when Clancy followed the movement. The old man was as sharp as all get out and Kent didn't like the speculation suddenly rife in the older man's eyes. Or the smile that curved his lips.

'Have you lived in Martin's Gully all your life, Clancy?'

'Aye, lass.'

'I bet you've some stories you could tell.'

Kent could see Josie would love to hear each and every one of them.

'That I could.' Clancy's gaze darted from Josie to Kent and back again. 'How are you finding the hospitality at Eagle Reach?'

Josie's lips twitched and her eyes met Kent's again. 'Improving.'

Great. Wonderful. He knew exactly what Clancy would make of that.

As expected, Clancy raised a telling eyebrow and Kent found himself leaping to his feet. He didn't care what the gossips like Bridget Anderson thought, but he did care what Clancy thought. And he wanted Clancy to unthink it right now.

'Kent?'

Josie's breathy whisper brought him back. 'It's time I was going.' He pulled the brim of his hat down low on his forehead. 'I want to check on Liz before I head back.'

'I hear she's poorly. Give her my love.'

Kent nodded then strode off, though he didn't know whose gaze burned through him the hotter—Clancy's or Josie's.

* * *

Josie pulled her gaze from Kent's rigid, rapidly retreating back and smiled at Clancy.

Clancy's eyes were knowing. He nodded after Kent. 'He's a good lad.'

Good? Lad? More like maddening man. Not that that did justice to the clamour Kent created inside her either, but she nodded all the same. Kent obviously looked out for Clancy and she had to give him credit for that. In fact, it was right neighbourly of him. 'He saved me from a day of servitude behind one of the stalls.' That was right neighbourly too.

Clancy chuckled. 'Bridget Anderson got her claws into you, did she? She's a managing kind of woman, that one. Likes to run things. She should've gone into politics.'

Josie laughed at the idea, but it was perfect. She wondered if Clancy could come up with a vocation as appropriate for her?

'How are you enjoying your holiday at Eagle Reach?'

Her hesitation betrayed her. 'I… It's a bit lonely.' She shrugged. 'I mean, it is beautiful—the bush, the river, and I've never seen night skies quite like it.' She didn't want Clancy thinking she didn't appreciate it. 'I just… I don't think I'm cut out for so much solitude.'

'Aye.' Clancy nodded. 'Neither is Kent.'

She sat back so fast she nearly fell off her seat. 'Are you serious?'

His eyes twinkled for a moment then they sobered. 'Aye, lass.'

'But…' She floundered with the idea. 'He's so rugged and strong and…hard. He doesn't look as if it bothers him at all.' She frowned. 'In fact, he seems jealous of it, doesn't want anything encroaching on it.' Especially her.

'Ahh…'

But Clancy didn't add anything and Josie refused to pry. The older man's eyes did watch her closely though, speculation rife in their depths, and she suddenly realised why Kent had left so abruptly. It made her want to laugh. Then it didn't.

Clancy was the one person she'd met in Martin's Gully who cared about Kent. Their mutual respect, their friendship, had been evident from the first moment. She reached across the table and touched the older man's hand. 'I'm only here for three more weeks. Kent thinks I'm a lame duck. Believe me, he'll be glad to see the back of me.'

Clancy chuckled. 'That's what he wants you to think.' He patted her hand. 'Now, why don't you come visit an old man next time you're in town?'

'I'd love to.'

'That's my place there.'

He nodded to a neat weatherboard house across the road and Josie beamed. The next three weeks were starting to look brighter and brighter.

Josie tried to slow her heart rate as she raised her hand and knocked on Kent's back door. 'Hi,' she said when he appeared. She tried to grin but found her lips had gone as rubbery as her knees.

He eyed her for a moment. 'Hi.'

No scowl, not even a frown, just a wary caution. Relief slugged through her. She hoped she'd seen the last of the prickly, unfriendly Kent. She much preferred the laughing, teasing one.

He glanced behind her. 'Is everything OK?'

'Yes, of course; I…'

He'd forgotten. She wanted to stamp her feet. She wanted to slap him. She wanted to cry with irrational disappointment. She'd looked forward to this all day, and…and he'd forgotten.

She didn't stamp her feet. She didn't slap him. She didn't cry. She kept right on trying to smile. 'It's Monday.'

His eyes narrowed and travelled over her face as if searching for signs of sunstroke. 'That's right,' he said slowly, as if agreeing with a child.

Which didn't help her eradicate those childish impulses. She pulled in a breath and counted to three. 'You said you'd give me a chess lesson.'

He slapped a hand to his forehead and scowled. Josie took two steps back. 'Don't do that,' she hollered, keeping a tight rein on feet that itched to stamp and hands that burned to slap.

His scowl deepened. 'Do what?'

'Look like that, turn back into Mr Hyde.' Pride lifted her chin. 'I know you're not my nursemaid, I know you're not even my friend, but we can at least be civil to each other and enjoy a game of chess, can't we?'

'Sure we can.'

'We had a nice time yesterday.'

'Yep.'

She wished he'd show a bit more enthusiasm.

He shuffled his feet. 'So, no chocolate cake?' He smiled, but it didn't reach his eyes.

'Umm, no.' She'd hummed and hawed over that for ages. Then she'd remembered his reaction the last time she'd brought afternoon tea. 'Didn't you have enough of it yesterday?'

'Not on your life.'

This time the smile made it all the way to his eyes and Josie found herself breathing easier. 'Next Monday,' she promised.

* * *

He should've found a way to get out of this.

Josie stood there in a pair of white cargo shorts and a jade-green tank-top and she looked better than chocolate cake. She looked better than anything he'd seen in a long, long time. He had the distinct feeling the less time he spent in her company, though, the better. She made him want things he'd forced himself to forget. But as he stared down into her half-hopeful, half-fearful face, he couldn't turn her away. He'd promised.

'Why don't we sit out here?' He nodded to the seating on his veranda. He didn't want to sit in the kitchen, didn't want her scent clogging up his senses and wafting through his house so the first thing he smelt when he woke in the morning was her.

With a shrug she took a seat, stared out at him from her gold-flecked eyes then crossed her legs. Jeez! She couldn't be more than a hundred and sixty centimetres, tops, but she had legs that went on forever. He turned and stumbled back into the house, tossed a critical glance around the kitchen then scowled. The real reason he didn't want her in here was so he didn't have to hear any more about his lack of homeliness. That still stung.

'Smile,' she ordered when he reappeared with the chess set, dimpling herself.

He did his best to tutor his face into a bland mask. Yesterday he'd found it too easy to smile with Josie, too easy to laugh. It wasn't a habit he intended to cultivate. Women like Josie were best protected from men like him.

Chess lesson. They'd concentrate on the chess lesson. 'How well can you play?' He sighed when she stared at him blankly. 'How much do you know?'

'I know how the pieces move.'

It was a starting point.

Forty minutes later, Kent came to the conclusion that Josie was a terrible chess player. She seemed to have a constitutional aversion to seizing her opponent's pieces. Or, for that matter, giving up any of her own. He attacked. She retreated, trying to find a way to save every single pawn. She didn't understand the concept of sacrificing a piece for the greater good. She didn't have an attacking bone in her body.

Nice body, though.

Stop it. Focus on the chess. Don't go noticing...other stuff.

Problem was, he'd spent the entire chess lesson noticing other stuff. Noticing how still her hands were between plays. How small and shapely they were. Noticing how she caught her bottom lip between her teeth as she attempted to decipher the complexities of the game. Noticing how her skin had started to take on a golden glow after a week of being out in the sun.

Her tank-top outlined a shape that had his hands clenching into fists beneath the table. He'd deliberately angled his chair so he couldn't see her legs. He knew they were there, though. He bet she'd feel like silk. Warm silk. He wondered if he could ask her to wear something long-sleeved and shapeless next time. And a bag over her head.

Get a grip. He'd lost his marbles. Too much time in her company had addled his brain.

He shifted in his chair. Fat lot of good it'd do him anyway. It wouldn't matter how many layers she wore, they couldn't hide the unconscious grace of her hand movements. Even when he closed his eyes against the tug of her body, he could still smell her.

She didn't even chatter away at him, which was a darn shame because inane chatter always got on his nerves.

And if she got on his nerves it might distract him from her more…from other things. But no, he wasn't to be given even that salve. She sat there, hands folded on the table, eyes intent on the game, perfectly relaxed, perfectly at ease. Perfectly happy to keep her mouth-watering lips curved in a smile without offering up so much as one inane remark.

With something midway between a sigh of frustration and a groan of relief, Kent moved his queen in front of her king. 'Checkmate.'

Very gently, Josie laid her oak-tree king on its side then looked at all her pieces lined up on Kent's side of the table. 'I may not know a great deal about chess, but you just smashed me, didn't you?'

'Yep.'

'I'm pretty terrible, aren't I?'

'Yep.' If he was lucky she might give it up as a bad joke. Especially if he didn't encourage her.

'I'll get better with practice.'

Damn.

She angled her cute little chin at him. Double damn.

She motioned to the chessboard. 'Do you want any help packing up?'

'No.'

'Well, thanks for the game.' She leapt up and, with a little wave, sauntered off. If Kent didn't know better he'd swear pique rather than relief needled through him. He opened his mouth to call something after her then snapped it shut.

Seizing the game board, he stomped inside, his shoulders as stiff and wooden as one of his chess pieces.

* * *

'Which way, Molly?'

Molly panted and pushed herself against Josie's legs when Josie paused at the juncture of the path, but didn't indicate which direction she'd prefer.

Josie pursed her lips. They'd explored downriver last week. So, should they cross the river or explore upstream? She lifted her face to the sun, revelling in its warmth, noted the shade on the other side of the river and promptly made her decision. 'Upriver today, Molly. What do you say?'

Molly's tail wagged harder, making Josie laugh. If anyone heard the way she spoke to the dog they'd think she was certifiable. She'd begun to look forward to her daily walks, though. They might have started out as a way to kill time, but she could feel her body reaping the benefits of regular exercise. Since she'd been practically housebound for the last few months, it felt good to work her muscles and drag fresh, clean air into her lungs. She'd continue the walks when she got home too.

And she'd get a dog.

She and Molly walked for about ten minutes before the trees started to thin and the river widened and grew shallow, creating a natural ford. Boulders dotted the river and both banks. The splashing of water and the glint of sun off mini-rapids and the pleasant browns and reds of the river stone created a scene that charmed her.

Until she heard a deeper splash immediately up ahead behind another group of boulders.

She didn't like big noises. That kind of splash indicated an animal at least as big as Molly. Were there wild pigs out here? She didn't know and didn't want to find out. She started to back up. 'C'mon, Molly, time to…'

She didn't get to finish her sentence because Molly,

with a bark, charged ahead. Oh, lord. Josie groaned and took off after her. What on earth would she say to Kent if anything happened to Molly?

No way was she skirting around the boulders as Molly had, though. Josie scrambled on top of them, hoping for a height advantage, readying herself to wave her arms and holler her lungs out in an effort to appear as big and scary as possible to whatever was below.

She wound up for her first holler when… 'Hello, Josie.'

Josie nearly fell into the river. 'Kent!'

Below her, Kent trod water in a natural pool formed by the boulders. Something midway between a scowl and a grimace darted across his face. Water glistened off his hair and his tanned, broad shoulders, and Josie's heart started to pound. She had a startlingly erotic image of licking those water droplets from his body, and the breath hitched in her throat. The water was clear, but the lower portion of his body was hidden by the shadow cast by the boulders.

Good thing!

When Josie didn't answer him Kent shaded his eyes and stared up at her. He must've noticed the colour in her cheeks, the way her eyes bugged, because a slow smile tilted one corner of his mouth. 'Earth to Josie.'

She started and rushed to cover her confusion. 'I, umm, heard a splash.'

'And you decided to investigate?'

'Umm, no.' She scrambled down from the boulder before she fell off. From the bank she couldn't see any part of Kent below the water line, but if she moved a little to her left and took a step forward—

Arghh! She hauled herself back and promptly sat on a

rock, and tried to quell the outrageous impulses coursing through her. She wrapped her arms around her knees to stop them trembling. 'No, umm…'

She grasped around for her train of thought, found it, and started to breathe easier once again. 'It sounded like a big splash, so I was going to slink back the way I'd come.' She sent him an apologetic grimace. 'Afraid I'm not interested in bumping into a hippopotamus or polar bear or anything.'

His smile became a grin. 'Last time I checked, they didn't do real well in the Australian wild.'

His grin was infectious. 'You know what I mean.' She grinned back. 'A wild pig or something.'

'You're pretty safe around here, but up a tree is a seriously good option if you ever do come across one. OK?'

'OK.' She filed the information away.

'So how come you decided to investigate?'

'Molly took off up here.'

'And you figured it was safe?'

She wanted to slap a hand to her forehead. Of course it was safe. Molly was a bigger scaredy cat than Josie. She must've smelt Kent or something. She wouldn't have gone racing off into danger. Josie suddenly felt like the biggest idiot on the planet. 'Umm,' she moistened her lips, 'that's right.'

Kent threw his head back and laughed. 'Liar. You thought Molly needed protecting, didn't you?'

She hitched up her chin. 'What's wrong with that?

He shook his head and grinned. 'Josie, you're a hopeless case, you know that?'

But he said it so nicely she didn't care. 'This is a lovely spot.' She lifted her face to the sun and glanced around with half-closed eyes, took in the clothes tossed on a nearby rock—shirt, jeans…underpants. Her eyes widened. 'Are you skinny-dipping, Mr Black?'

'I most certainly am, Ms Peterson.'

Warmth and wistfulness squirmed through her in equal measure. She bet it was lovely, the cool silk of water flowing over you without impediment. The freedom of it. 'I've never skinny-dipped in my life.'

He smiled challengingly and waggled his eyebrows. 'Wanna try it?'

He should do that more. Smile. It softened the craggy lines of his face and made him look like a man she could—

Nonsense! Crazy thought. She smiled and settled back on her sun-warmed rock. 'No, thank you.' Her smile widened. 'Though I might take it up as a spectator sport.'

Ooh, yes, definitely some ogling potential here. Not that she needed to see more than his shoulders and arms. He had biceps that could hurl a girl's heart rate right off the chart.

'If you don't stop looking at me like that I'm going to pull you in here to cool off.'

He practically growled the words at her and their former teasing banter vanished, replaced by a hot and heavy awareness. Heat surged through her…and not just in her cheeks. For one heart-stopping moment she was tempted to keep ogling and see what happened.

Another crazy thought. If he pulled her in there with him neither one of them would cool off. She tried to school her face. 'Sorry.'

'I'm going to get out now.'

Her mouth watered. 'Uh-huh.'

'Would you like to turn around?'

Her lips twitched at the gentleness of the question. 'Why, Kent Black, are you embarrassed?'

'No.' He held her gaze. 'But I thought you might be.'

He started to rise and with a squawk she leapt off her rock and spun around, heart pounding. His chuckle made it that much harder to keep from turning around. She could imagine what she'd see. All too vividly. She forced herself to take several paces upstream. Away from temptation. Or, at least, another couple of big rocks from it.

If only she was the kind of woman who could indulge in a holiday romance, in transitory affairs.

Her heart slapped against her ribcage. Her mind suddenly whirled. Well, why couldn't she? She was on holiday, wasn't she? She wanted to change her life, didn't she? Maybe that meant taking a few risks.

And if it meant seeing Kent naked…

She didn't think twice, she swung back to face him. Ooh…jockey shorts—navy blue—plastered to—

Oh, God! She couldn't drag her eyes away from the evidence of his arousal.

'What do you think you're doing?' Kent shouted at her, his eyes starting from his head.

She tried to stop her heart from thudding right out of her chest. Oh, dear lord. The man was beautiful. The air in front of her eyes shimmered with heat. He wanted her. That much was obvious. And exhilarating. It gave her the courage to hitch up her chin and meet his gaze. 'I've changed my mind.'

'About?'

'Seeing you naked.'

'You what?'

'So couldn't we take it from the top?' She took a step towards him. 'I'd love to try skinny-dipping.'

He stabbed a finger at her. He glared. 'You stay right where you are.'

His eyes darkened when she ignored him, when she moved in so close she could watch the pulse pounding at the base of his throat. She wanted to touch her tongue to it.

'You don't know what you're doing.' His voice rasped out of his throat. His chest rose and fell.

'I know exactly what I'm doing.' She reached out and placed her hand over his heart. He stiffened, but he didn't step back. His skin was cool and firm. The blood pounded beneath her palm, making her tremble.

'Think, Josie, think!' The words rapped out of him like stone on tin. 'You're not a holiday-fling kind of person. You couldn't stop it from meaning too much. I've met women like you before.'

Still…he didn't step away.

'You'd smother me, I'd fight for space,' his voice grew ragged, 'we'd argue, you'd cry.' He pulled in a breath. 'It'd get complicated and I don't do complicated.'

'Complicated? How?'

'You said you couldn't live out here and I can't live anywhere else.'

Can't or won't? But she let it pass. Beneath her hand his heart pounded hard and fast.

'Too complicated,' he repeated, but she noted the way his jaw clenched, the way his eyes flared with desire.

'On the contrary, it's remarkably simple.' She reached out and took his right hand, placed it between her breasts so he could feel her heart racing too. 'I want to touch you, and I want you to touch me.' The warmth of his hand pressed into her. She arched against it. Her lips parted. 'What's complicated about that?'

The words had barely left her when, with a wild oath, Kent swung an arm around her waist and his mouth crashed down on hers. His urgency, the hardness of his arousal against her stomach, fired her with an answering urgency, with a hunger she hadn't known she possessed, hadn't even known existed.

His tongue swept across her inner lips, enticed her to tangle her tongue with his, and turned everything topsy-turvy. The shoulders, the rock-hard body she clung to, though, stayed upright and held her fast, one hand at her hip, the other tangled in her hair, urging her closer.

He broke off to press hot kisses to her throat before claiming her mouth again. Their desire swept her along like a swollen current of the river, like gale-force winds that bent the tops of trees. She felt wild, free…cherished. She—

'No!'

Kent jerked back and glared. Through the haze of her desire she saw the torment in his eyes. His fingers bit into her shoulders and he shook her, but she had a feeling it was himself he wanted to shake. She made a move to reach out to him, to try and wipe away the pain that raked his face, but he dropped his hands and stepped back out of her reach.

'This is not going to happen,' he ground out.

Her arms felt bereft, cold. She gulped. Need lapped at her. 'Don't you want me?' she whispered. What had she done wrong?

A laugh scraped out of Kent's throat. He shoved his hands into opposite armpits and gripped for dear life. 'Don't play the ingénue. You can't be blind to the effect you have on men.'

The effect she had on…

What? Her? A smile suddenly zipped through her. Kent backed up as if he'd seen and recognised the glint in her eyes. He seized his jeans and shoved his legs into them bending over as he pulled on his boots.

'Nice butt,' she offered.

He glared, pushed his arms into his chambray shirt.

'Ditto for the shoulders.'

He growled but she couldn't make out what he said. It sounded like 'crazy thinking' and something about a mouse, which didn't make any sense at all.

He seized his hat, slapped it against his thigh and strode off without saying another word. Josie watched him until he disappeared into the trees then she dropped to her knees and buried her face in Molly's fur. 'He wants me,' she whispered. She couldn't temper the jubilation that rushed through her, didn't try to.

He wanted her. He just needed some time to get used to the idea. That was all.

CHAPTER SEVEN

JOSIE didn't clap eyes on Kent again till Friday. Three whole days since that kiss by the river. And it wasn't for lack of trying. She'd kept her eyes peeled for sight of him, whilst her imagination played any number of fantasies through her mind. Lovely, provocative fantasies.

Three days. She'd tried to keep a lid on her impatience, reminded herself he needed time.

Then on Friday, when she pulled up in her car after visiting Clancy, she glanced up to find Kent striding towards her cabin. He wore an expression of such single-minded determination that her heart started to hammer. Oh, man, had he finally come to his senses? She leapt out of her car, her knees barely holding her up.

Then she saw the bucket and broom in his hands and her heart plummeted. He wasn't looking for her. He wasn't heading for her cabin, but the one next door. He had no intention of sweeping her up in his arms and kissing her senseless.

Across a distance of twenty feet or so, they stopped and stared at each other like adversaries in an old-fashioned gun draw, each waiting for the other to make a move.

She swallowed back her disappointment...and impatience…brought their kiss to the forefront of her mind and grinned. Kent could act as aloof and distant as he wanted. She knew better. And she had no intention of making things easy for him. She sent him a cheery wave. 'Hey, Kent. Want a coffee?'

He tipped his hat in answer and bolted.

Her mouth dropped open and, unbidden, tears blurred her vision as a shaft of pain skewered her to the spot. In that moment she saw with startling clarity what she'd refused to see before. Kent had been right. If she couldn't stop a kiss from meaning too much, how would she cope with making love with him? She sagged against the bonnet of her car. How could she walk away at the end of her holiday if they made love?

She wouldn't, that was what. And Kent knew it. She'd cling; he'd rebel. She'd cry; he'd hate himself. A shudder racked through her. Dear lord, what had she been thinking?

Quite obviously she hadn't been thinking at all. But no matter how many times she listed all the reasons why it was a bad idea to make love with Kent, her wayward body went right on trying to imagine it anyway.

The last three days had created a gentle rhythm to Josie's days. She'd wake early, have her first cup of coffee on the veranda with Molly and the birds, then she'd bake up a batch of muffins and a cake, or some biscuits and a tart, and drive into Martin's Gully to the general store.

She'd met Liz on Monday, recovered from the worst of her flu, and had immediately warmed to the other woman. She understood why Kent held her in such high esteem. Liz Perkins had a kind heart and not a bad word for anybody. So, naturally, Josie, Liz and Bridget breakfasted together over muffins and a pot of tea.

Then it was home again to wash her pots and pans, tidy her cabin, and to read the day's paper. As soon as any disquieting thought popped into her head she'd quickly push it aside. She'd decided the question of what to do with the rest of her life could wait until the middle of next week. She'd have a go at sorting it all out then, but she'd resolved on at least two weeks of complete relaxation first.

Then it was back into Martin's Gully for lunch with Clancy, a habit she was hardly aware of forming, but one she enjoyed all the same. Once home again, she and Molly would go for their walk.

Most of the time, throughout the day, Josie could push thoughts of Kent from her mind. Mostly. Sure, it required the occasional concerted effort, but she managed it. The nights, though, were a different matter.

As soon as evening fell another woman seemed to inhabit her body. A reckless, wanton woman who wanted nothing more than to stride up to Kent's back door in something skimpy and seductive and demand entry. No number of craft projects, no amount of postcard writing could drive the ensuing images out of her mind.

When sleep finally claimed her, she tossed and turned and groaned until Molly's whine or bark woke her. Then she'd surge upright, erotic images branded on her brain, her skin fevered with need.

Molly took to sleeping on the floor rather than the foot of Josie's bed. Josie didn't blame her. She'd sleep on the floor too if she thought it'd help.

Saturday morning Josie woke with a cough and a pain behind her eyes. She ignored it and carried on as normal.

Sunday morning she dragged herself out of bed, pulled muffin ingredients off the shelves then remembered it was

Sunday and she didn't need to bake today. She let Molly out, crawled back into bed and pulled the covers over her head. Today she'd hibernate.

Kent woke at two o'clock in the morning to whining and scratching outside his bedroom window. Then Molly set up a howl. 'For Pete's sake!' He threw back the covers, muttering imprecations under his breath as he lurched to the front door and flung it open. Who'd ever heard of a dog afraid of the dark? 'C'mon, then,' he grumbled.

Molly didn't try to bowl him over with ecstatic wriggling and licks the way she normally did. She barked at him then turned her head in the direction of the cabins.

In the direction of Josie's cabin.

It might be two o'clock in the morning and he might be fuzzy-headed, but Kent didn't need a second signal. He jumped through the door, realised he was stark naked, raced back inside to pull on jeans and a shirt, dragged on his trainers and slammed out of the house to race after Molly.

Fear surged through him. His heart grew so large it pressed against his lungs, making him battle for every breath. Let her be OK. Let her be OK. The words pounded through him with each step.

Her cabin was all lit up and he didn't hesitate to catch his breath. He didn't hesitate for anything. He pounded on her door then tried it. Locked. He peered through the window but the curtains obscured his view. He pounded on the door again. 'Josie!' He rattled the handle. If she didn't answer he'd break the damn thing down. 'Josie!'

His shout should've woken the dead. From inside he heard a groan then a soft shuffling… The door opened. He took one look at her face and pity, tenderness and concern punched him. She looked terrible. She looked worse than terrible.

She blinked and clutched the doorframe, rested her head against it. 'What can I do for you?'

He could hardly make out the words as they rasped from her throat. Didn't she realise this wasn't a social call? That it was two o'clock in the morning? Another rush of tenderness took him off guard. 'Sweetheart, I think you'll find you're not well.'

She swayed and he leapt forward, slid an arm around her waist and moved her back to sit on the end of the sofa bed. She felt small and frail beneath his hands, her skin clammy and hot. She was burning up.

'Might be why I don't feel too good,' she slurred.

She went to lie back down but he stopped her, so she leaned into him instead. Even sick she still smelt good enough to eat. 'I promise to let you go back to sleep, as soon as you've answered a couple of questions.' She gave no indication she'd heard him, so he placed a finger beneath her chin and lifted her face towards him. 'Josie?'

'I'm wearing my silly, skimpy pyjamas.' Her mouth turned down. 'I should get my robe.'

He had a feeling she felt too tired and sick to care about the robe, but he wished she hadn't drawn attention to her nightwear. He'd done his best not to notice. Her pyjamas consisted of pale pink short shorts and a singlet top covered in fluffy white sheep jumping fences.

Corny. Cute. And in other circumstances downright sexy. He fought the bolt of need that shot through him. 'I promise to tease you about them when you're well again.' Her lips twitched into what he guessed was meant to be a smile. 'Now, tell me where it hurts most.'

'Chest,' she wheezed. 'It's hard to breathe.'

'Are you an asthmatic?'

She shook her head and leaned further into him until her head rested fully against his shoulder. Her face lifted towards his, her eyes closed.

'Josie.' He cupped her face and felt her glands. Swollen. 'I want you to open your mouth and stick out your tongue.'

She opened one eye then lifted one hand and waggled a finger at him. 'Trust me, right? I'm a doctor.'

He smiled. He couldn't help it. He couldn't believe she'd try and crack a joke when she obviously felt so bad. He fought the urge to kiss her forehead. 'That's the one.'

If only she knew.

None the less, she did as he asked. He angled her face to the light. He could smell the infection on her breath but a quick look at her throat confirmed it.

She had a throat and chest infection. And a fever. She needed antibiotics. She needed to keep hydrated. And she needed sleep. He helped her back under the covers. 'When did you last eat?'

But she'd drifted down under cover of sleep and he knew he wouldn't get any more from her tonight. He poured a glass of water, noticed the remains of a barely touched bowl of soup and drew his own conclusions. He made her drink several mouthfuls of the water.

'Stay,' he ordered Molly, who lay on a rug at the base of the sofa bed. Rug? He shook the thought away then strode back up to the house, seized a jar of broad-spectrum antibiotics from his bag, the night lamp from beside his bed then headed straight back down to the cabin.

He made her take two tablets and another couple of sips of water before cooling her forehead with a cold cloth.

Then he set the lamp up on the table, flicked off the overhead light and settled down to keep vigil.

Josie had that dream again. That lovely dream where Kent leaned over her, his face softened in concern, his hands gentle on her face and beautifully cool. This time the room was bathed in a gentle light rather than the harsh light above her head. She tried to smile at him, tried to say she thought him wonderful…and sexy, but her body felt mired in thick mud and she couldn't manage it.

Then a jag of coughing shook through her entire frame and each breath felt like broken glass and it took all her concentration to breathe through it. For a moment she swore a pair of strong arms lifted her and supported her, but then everything went black as a deeper sleep claimed her.

The next time Kent entered her dreams she wanted him to get right back out of them again. Why couldn't she dream what she wanted to dream? Why couldn't they be floating down a wide, slow river on a beautiful, cushion-strewn pontoon, or lying in a field of wild flowers with the sky blue above them, listening to the lazy hum of the bees?

Sure, he was still as sexy as ever with a smile made for sin, and he smelt better than any man had a right to, but he was also annoying. She didn't want to take tablets and drink water. Why wouldn't he stop making her? She couldn't avoid him, though. He wouldn't let her. His big hands and superior strength mocked her efforts to elude him.

The dream was all the more annoying because in it she was as weak as a kitten and her brain was too fuzzy to bring into play her self-defence tactics. By the time she remembered the right move, she found herself lying back down on the pillow with a gentle hand soothing her forehead and she couldn't remember what she'd wanted to fight against.

Dreams were like that.

Josie opened one eye, noticed the soft light pouring in at the windows and realised she'd slept later than she'd meant to or, at least, later than she normally did. She pulled a tentative breath into her lungs. Her chest still hurt, but the sharp, broken-glass pains had dulled to an ache. A definite improvement.

She pulled herself slowly upright, pushed her hair off her face then froze. Kent sat half-slumped in one of the hard chairs at the kitchen table, fast asleep. What was he doing here? Then she remembered fragments from her dreams and wondered if they'd been dreams at all. She frowned. She had the faintest recollection of opening her door to him at some stage last night.

Molly lumbered to her feet from her rug on the floor, stretched and yawned. When she saw Josie she gave a joyful bark. Kent was on his feet in seconds. Josie had never seen anyone move so fast in her life. Certainly not like that, from sleep to wakefulness in an instant.

He was at her side in seconds, his hand at her forehead, his eyes intent on her face. 'How do you feel?'

'Crappy,' she groaned.

He broke out into a huge grin.

'I'm glad you find it amusing,' she grumbled, throwing back the covers and reaching for her robe.

The smile slid right off his face. 'What do you think you're doing?'

'Gotta make the muffins,' she wheezed. Liz would be expecting them.

'No, you're not.'

He seized her feet and lifted them straight back into bed, and Josie found herself too weak to fight him. In fact, she found it took most of her energy just to breathe. He tucked the covers around her and sat on the edge of the bed. Luckily, she didn't have the energy to pull him down to kiss her either. She gripped her hands tightly in her lap all the same, just in case she found a sudden second wind.

'You're not getting out of bed at all today.'

'But—'

'Doctor's orders.'

She snapped her mouth shut. Then she frowned. 'The doctor's been to see me?'

He hesitated then nodded. 'Yep.'

She didn't remember that at all. 'Could you...?' She twisted her hands together. She hated putting him out like this. 'Could you ring Liz and explain that—?'

'Already taken care of.'

It was? She glanced at the light filtering through the curtains. 'But it can't even be eight o'clock yet.'

'Twenty to,' he confirmed with a glance at his watch.

'Heavens! What time did you call her?' A spurt of indignation shuffled through her. What right did he have to take matters into his own hands?

Then she remembered he was only following the doctor's orders. 'I... Thank you.'

A frown drew his brows low over the brilliant blue of his eyes, tightening then deepening the groove that ran from his nose to the side of his mouth. Her chest, already clenched, clenched up more until she realised he hadn't directed the frown at her, but at the wall behind her. 'What day of the week do you think it is?'

An awful premonition shook her. 'Monday, of course.' Though she suddenly realised there was no 'of course' about it. If she couldn't recall a visit from the doctor, then…

'You've been quite sick, Josie.'

'What kind of sick?'

He folded his arms and glared in the direction of the sink. As long as he didn't glare at her she didn't mind.

'You have a chest infection.'

Uh-huh. 'What day is it?'

He rubbed a hand across the back of his neck then glanced at her through the lock of hair that fell forward on his forehead. 'Thursday.'

'Thursday!' She surged upright, found it hard to breathe again and subsided back against the pillows. How could she have lost three days just like that? Another thought spiked through her. She didn't jump up and wring her hands, although she wanted to. Her mouth went dry. 'Have you been looking after me all that time?'

He nodded and she wanted to cover her face with her hands and curl up into a ball. 'I'm sorry.'

'No big deal.'

No big deal. He was joking, right? It was a huge deal. *Had he seen her naked?* The thought spiked through her and she wanted to die. 'Serves you right for that crack you made last week about not being my nursemaid,' she suddenly snapped. 'You shouldn't tempt fate like that.'

He blinked then grinned. 'You're going to be one of those grumbling, sniping, griping patients, huh?'

She covered her mouth with her hand. 'I'm sorry.'

'Nah, it serves me right.'

It did?

She shook her head. 'I know how much you hate being…
I mean, I'm sorry I've been such a nuisance. I wouldn't
have put you to so much trouble for the world.'

He reached out and clasped her hand, his eyes gentle.
'I'm quite sure you'd have much preferred to stay healthy.'

He leaned back with that grin and her mouth watered.
She suddenly found it hard to breathe leaning back against
the pillows too.

'So, as penance, I have to spend the next three days playing
chess with the worst chess player in the history of man.'

Josie stared then laughed. It ended in a fit of
coughing. Kent's arms came around her and held her
steady until it finished. Finally she drew back, just far
enough to stare up into his face, to take in the lean,
tempting line of his lips. He needed a shave and she
wondered how it'd feel to run her palm along the length
of his jaw.

Kent released her and shot to his feet, shoved his hands
in his pockets. 'Time for you to rest.'

Then she remembered the way he'd raced away from her
that day by the river, and how he'd avoided her ever since.

How he didn't want her on his mountain.

'Is that how long I have to stay in bed?' Is that what the
doctor had ordered? 'Three days?'

'At the very least.'

She couldn't continue being such a drain on him for
another three days, but she found it hard to focus that
thought as her eyes fought against the sleep that suddenly
wanted to claim her. 'I can't possibly stay here.'

'Sure you can.'

No, she couldn't. But her eyes closed and she found she
didn't have the strength to push the words past her throat.

* * *

Fabulous. Wonderful.

Kent dragged a hand down his face. It'd been hard enough dealing with a Josie who was out of it. Having to touch her, hold her, whilst he administered antibiotics and made her sip water. Having to steel himself against the desire that coursed through him when he sponged her down, when he changed the sheets. Whenever he darn well looked at her. Having to fight the urge to kiss her when, in her delirium, she told him she dreamed of making love with him.

He despised himself for his weakness, for not being able to view her as just another patient. His lips twisted. So much for maintaining a professional distance.

He dragged a hand down his face. A sleeping Josie had strained all his reserves of self-control and discipline, but a waking one was that much more potent again. He didn't know how he'd get through the next few days.

'What about your cows?' Josie asked the next time he moved to sit on the edge of her bed.

'Steers,' he corrected. He hadn't realised she was awake. He hadn't wanted to wake her either, but it was time she ate something. She eased herself up into a sitting position. He propped the pillows behind her.

'Who's looking after them?'

He suppressed a grin. He should've known it wouldn't take her long to get around to that. 'Smiley McDonald. A neighbour. We have an arrangement.'

She eyed him doubtfully. 'You do?'

'Yep.' He slid a tray holding a bowl of soup and a couple of slices of toast onto her lap.

'Which is?'

When she didn't pick up her spoon and start eating, he

put the spoon into her hand. 'Smiley hangs his head over our boundary fence and checks on my cattle. If there's a problem he takes care of it, or calls the vet, or lets me know. I'm returning the favour next month when he attends his sister's wedding in Adelaide.'

'Oh.'

She started to eat and he moved to the hard chair by the table. When she finished he cleared the tray and returned with a glass of water and a pill. 'Antibiotics,' he said when she hesitated.

'Thank you.' She took it without a murmur. 'Thank you for lunch and thank you for taking such good care of me.'

She smiled and in that instant he swore it was all worthwhile. 'Not a problem.' He retreated to the sink, out of temptation's way. Or at least out of its reach for the moment.

'Yes, it is. You said it's three days before I can get back up.'

He swung around sharply, not liking the tone of her voice. 'You won't be able to do too much all at once.' He didn't want her overdoing it. 'You'll need to take it pretty easy for a couple of weeks.'

'But—'

'There are no buts. Not if you don't want a relapse.'

She huddled back against the pillows and bit her lip. He wanted to pull her into his arms and tell her it'd all be OK. She just needed to take it easy, that was all. He bet she wasn't used to taking it easy. He had a feeling that over the last few months she'd taken care of her father at the expense of her own health. He didn't like that thought. Why hadn't her brothers looked out for her? He straddled the chair and tried not to scowl. He'd make sure she took it easy.

'I can't trespass on your kindness for that long.'

'Sure you can.'

'It's not fair on you. You have your work and other responsibilities.'

No, he didn't. Not real responsibilities like making a sick person well again. He'd forgotten what that felt like...and he missed it. He shrugged the thought aside. He'd chosen his path. 'Lots of things aren't fair.' It wasn't fair she was stuck halfway up a mountain on a holiday she didn't even want.

'I'll have to go home.'

Her voice was flat, matter-of-fact, and the words jarred through him. He leapt out of his chair, but then didn't know what he meant to do. Concern spiked through him when the colour drained from her face.

He closed the distance in an instant and felt her forehead—cool and dry. Her fever hadn't returned. Relief flooded him. 'Josie, you're not strong enough to drive home just yet.'

She met his gaze then glanced down to where her fingers pleated the blanket. 'I know, but if you rang Marty and Frank then they could come collect me.'

Marty and Frank wouldn't look after her as well as he could. If they were such good brothers, why had they sent her out to this God-forsaken spot in the first place, huh? He didn't want to let Josie out of his sight until he was one hundred per cent sure she was well again.

'Will they be able to look after you?' he fired at her.

'Of course.'

'Properly?'

'Yes.' She laughed but he caught the strain behind it. 'I think it'd be for the best, don't you?'

Her soft words speared through him and he wanted to

say no. But damn it. What could he offer her other than a rustic cabin, huh?

And a hard bed.

And tinned soup.

She hadn't wanted to stay when she was well, why would she want to stay now she was sick? She deserved all the comforts of home and she wouldn't get those even if he moved her up into the house. She should be taken care of and made a fuss of by her family and friends, the people who loved her. A circle that didn't include him.

His hands clenched. If that was what she wanted he'd make sure it happened. 'I'll do whatever you need me to,' he promised. 'Are you sure you wouldn't rather stay?'

She smiled but it didn't reach her eyes. 'You're not my nursemaid, remember?'

She didn't say it in a mean way to make him eat his words or anything, and that only made it worse. 'But—'

'We both know I'm someone you just got lumped with.'

'Not true.' He wished he'd been friendlier in the first week of her stay. He shifted awkwardly. 'You'll be missed.'

She raised an eyebrow and he found himself shrugging. 'Liz enjoys her morning cuppa with you. And I haven't seen Clancy looking so dapper in a long time.'

'Oh.' She gave a wan smile.

'And I was looking forward to thrashing you some more at chess.'

She sent him an even thinner, sadder excuse for a smile. 'I don't believe you.'

If he kissed her she'd believe him.

For Pete's sake! She's sick, you jerk.

On second thoughts, it was probably a good idea if she went home. A scowl scuffed through him, but he kept his face bland and pleasant. No, not pleasant. He couldn't do pleasant if his life depended on it. He could just about manage polite if he concentrated really hard.

He concentrated really hard then seized a notepad and pen and thrust them at her. 'If you write down their phone numbers I'll get on to it.'

He swung away to lean in the doorway and stare out at the view. He wanted to get out of the close confines of the cabin. Now. He needed to stride out beneath a big sky and breathe in fresh air.

When he swung back, he found Josie pale and trembling. He was at her side in the space of a heartbeat, but she refused to relinquish the notepad when he tried to take it. 'Rest,' he ordered, cursing himself for not keeping a closer eye on her. 'We'll deal with this later.'

She scribbled down the numbers, tore off the top page and handed it to him. 'I'll rest while you get on to this.'

She hunkered back down under the covers and turned her back to him. He didn't even try to keep the scowl from his face as he strode from the cabin.

He glanced down at the scrap of paper. She'd scrawled four phone numbers—home and business for Marty, home and business for Frank. He wanted to scrunch it up into a ball and throw it away. When she woke he could tell her she'd dreamt the whole incident, and that she was staying put until she was well again.

But he knew it wouldn't work. Josie wasn't delirious any more. She knew fact from fiction. She knew what she wanted.

She wanted to go home.

He slammed into the house. It seemed strangely grey after the touches of colour Josie had added to her cabin. His scowl deepened. Without giving himself time to think, he pulled the phone towards him and punched in the first number—Marty, business.

Ten minutes later he slammed the phone down. The sound echoed in the sudden silence.

Of all the miserable low-lifes! Once he'd discovered she wasn't sick enough for hospital, Marty Peterson had claimed he couldn't possibly collect Josie before Tuesday next week at the earliest.

Tuesday. That was five days away.

And he was dreadfully sorry for the inconvenience, but he'd make sure Mr Black was amply reimbursed for all the bother.

Bother! Kent snorted. Josie didn't need some jerk throwing money around. She needed family and friends and some wildly overdue pampering. What she didn't need was a miserable excuse for a brother who couldn't come and collect her because he had *very important work* to do.

Kent would give him very important work. If he ever clapped eyes on Marty Peterson he'd knock him flat on his back.

He punched in the business number for the second brother, Frank. They couldn't both be low-life scum. Josie was a sweetheart. At least one of her brothers had to share some of the same personality traits, surely?

A busy signal greeted him. He gripped the receiver so hard by rights it should've cracked. He slammed it down and swore once, loudly. What was the bet crappy brother number one was on the phone warning crappy brother number two?

He paced. These were the guys whose feelings Josie had wanted to protect by staying here and not complaining?

It took him forty-seven minutes to get through, but he

had no intention of giving up. Finally a secretary answered and informed him *regretfully* that Mr Peterson was away on a business trip, and would he like to leave a message?

The kind of message he wanted to leave would've blistered her ears and peeled the paint clean off the kitchen wall. He reminded himself not to shoot the messenger. With a curt, 'No,' he hung up.

What the heck was he going to tell Josie?

He had vivid, satisfying visions of beating both men to a pulp. Immature, he admitted, but still satisfying. He rubbed the back of his neck, his mind working overtime. He could drive Josie home himself. A round trip would take the best part of a day. No drama. He could drive her car then hire another for the return journey. At least he'd know she'd arrived safely. Three hours there, a couple of hours to see her settled, then three hours back again.

But what would she be going home to? He couldn't count on her brothers with their *very important work* to look after her. And she had that sick neighbour. He couldn't count on Josie looking after herself properly if she thought somebody needed her.

Nope, he wasn't taking her home. He might only be able to offer her a rustic cabin, but he could make sure she got the care she needed. That at least was something he could do. He reached for the phone and made another two calls, both far more satisfying than the earlier two. He actually found himself smiling at the end of them.

CHAPTER EIGHT

JOSIE must've dozed because when she next opened her eyes the sun had moved across the sky and the shadows outside her cabin were lengthening. She reached for her watch.

'Nearly four o'clock,' Kent said.

She couldn't believe how much she'd slept. A thought that slid right out of her head when she sat up and gazed at him. He sat sprawled at the table with one of her crossword books and he looked so good her mouth started to water. It was pointless all this wistful sighing and mouthwatering, but she couldn't seem to stop it.

The sooner she left the better. For both their sakes. She gulped and tried to make herself believe it. 'Did you—?'

'What's a five-letter word for food seasoning? The fourth letter is M.'

She tried to visualise the word. 'A food seasoning? No other letters yet?'

'I think four down is "astonish", so that would give us H as the second letter.'

'Something—H—something—M—something? I don't like it.' She held her hand out for the book. 'I bet you've made a mistake.'

He handed it to her then stretched out along the foot of

her bed and looked so darn sexy her eyes crossed, making it impossible to decipher the puzzle in front of her.

'Well?' He yawned.

'I can't make it out.' Wasn't that the truth?

He yawned again and guilt speared through her. She wondered how much sleep he'd managed in the last few days. Not much in those hard chairs, she'd bet.

She wanted to curl into a ball again and hide. The hairs on her arms lifted and her skin prickled whenever she thought about it. She opened her mouth to ask when Marty and Frank would be here, and something a whole lot greyer than guilt shuffled through her at the thought of leaving.

'Thyme,' she suddenly blurted out. 'T-H-Y-M-E. A food seasoning.'

Kent beamed at her and some of the greyness lifted. She'd ask about Marty and Frank right after she and Kent finished the crossword. But once they'd finished it, Kent stood and stretched, glanced around the cabin and she knew he was surveying the changes she'd made.

'Do you like it?'

He didn't pretend to misunderstand her. 'What's not to like? You've totally transformed the place.'

She snorted. 'Nonsense.'

'You have,' he insisted. 'The atmosphere in here is completely different.' He glanced around again, his brow furrowed. ' I can't even figure out what it is you've done exactly.'

'I've done nothing more than thrown a rug on the floor, a tablecloth on the table, and hung something cheerful at the windows.'

'What about that?' He pointed.

She shrugged. 'I hung a picture. Hardly an earth-shattering change.'

'And those?'

'They're just some candles I bought. They're supposed to smell like chocolate when you burn them.'

He was silent for a moment. 'You know, you might be right. Maybe I should do something...more with these cabins.'

Her jaw dropped. She wanted to throw her arms around him.

Bad, bad idea. What she should really be doing was asking him if he'd spoken to Marty.

But she couldn't seem to push the words out and in the end it was Kent who raised the subject first. 'Are you close to your brothers, Josie?'

'Why?' Her chin shot up, her back stiffened and she slammed the crossword book closed. 'What makes you ask?'

He raised his hands and backed up. 'No reason.'

She ordered herself to act less defensive, less...touchy.

'But they sent you out here to the back of beyond, didn't they?'

His voice was light, teasing, as if trying to put her at ease, and it roused all of her suspicions. 'Why, what did they say? You have spoken to them, haven't you?'

He shrugged. 'Only Marty so far.'

'And what—?'

'Knock, knock.'

Clancy stood in the doorway, an enormous bunch of flowers in one hand, an assortment of odds and ends in the other.

'How are you feeling, lass?' He placed the flowers in her arms.

'Oh, Clancy, they're beautiful.'

'Knew you'd like them. They're a bribe.'

'A bribe?'

'If you can't come to me for lunch then I'll just have to come to you.' His dark eyes twinkled. 'If you can fit me into your schedule, that is.'

She didn't even know if she'd be here for lunch tomorrow. She could be on her way home. 'Oh, Clancy, I...'

Kent shook his head wildly behind Clancy's back and Josie swallowed the rest of her words and pasted on a smile. 'Why, that sounds lovely.'

Clancy beamed his delight and guilt trickled through her. And regret. She'd miss him when she left.

She made a silent promise to have lunch with him tomorrow, although Marty and Frank wouldn't like the delay if they were here by then. Her insides shrank. In fact, they'd hate it. She steeled herself against tomorrow's inevitable argument and forced her attention back to Clancy. 'Though you're a little late for lunch today.'

'Oh, aye,' he agreed, setting up a folding table by her bed then taking her flowers and handing them to Kent. 'Make yourself useful, lad. Put those in water.' He disappeared back outside. Kent looked so charmingly nonplussed Josie had to laugh. The flowers did nothing to take the edge off his masculinity, though.

'I wanted to get in early and make it a date for the rest of the week before someone else snapped you up,' Clancy said, trundling back into the cabin with her camp chair and setting it by the folding table. 'Those others,' he nodded to the wooden chairs by her table, 'are too hard for old bones like mine.'

He set about brewing a large pot of tea, as at home in

her cabin as if born there. Kent managed to distribute the flowers between a single vase and a couple of jugs. Their fresh, clean scent filled the cabin. 'Clancy, you don't need to bribe me to have lunch with you.'

'They're not for lunch, lass, but for this.' He held up a pack of dominoes. 'Been feeling kind of dull over the last couple of days. Need a game or two to liven me up.'

Nonsense. He wanted to liven her up, keep her from being bored. His kindness touched her. But even she couldn't deny the enjoyment that coloured his cheeks and enlivened his eyes as he poured cups of tea, sliced a Boston bun and set out the dominoes.

He lifted his eyebrow at Kent, who hovered near by. 'I'm perfectly capable of looking after the patient. Don't you have work or something to do?' He held out the plate of Boston bun. 'Take a slice and be off with you.'

Josie choked back a laugh. Kent grinned. 'I can take a hint.'

Clancy's white hair danced. 'Smart man.'

A part of Josie followed Kent right out the door, wanting to dog his footsteps as he left. A bigger part of her wanted to throw her arms around Clancy and thank him. Kent probably needed a break. The less of a strain she proved to be the better.

Clancy stayed for just over an hour and left with promises to return for lunch tomorrow. He even left his folding table and dominoes. She stared at them and gulped. She had to find out what arrangements Kent had made with her brothers.

As if her thoughts had conjured him up, Kent stuck his head around the door. 'Worn out?'

'I'm fine.' She pulled in a deep breath. 'Kent, what—?'

'That was kindly done.'

She blinked. 'Oh, you mean it was kind of Clancy to come and visit?' Her face cleared. 'Of course it was and—'

'I meant exactly what I said.'

He folded his arms and the material of his T-shirt strained across his shoulders and the muscles of his upper arms. A great sigh rose up through her.

'He has one living relative. A nephew in Scotland. He's lonely. Visiting you made him feel needed.'

Josie didn't know what to say. 'I…I enjoy his company,' she finally managed.

'Exactly.'

'That's not kind, it's human.'

Kent took a step back and frustration pulsed through her, though she couldn't have said why. 'Look, Kent, what—?'

'Hello?' Footsteps sounded outside on the veranda and Liz appeared in the doorway, basket in hand.

'Come in,' Josie urged when she hovered there, staring from one to the other.

'Are you sure? Am I interrupting anything?'

Josie snorted though she wasn't sure why she did that either. She was aware of Kent's narrow-eyed gaze, though. 'You're not interrupting and visitors are always welcome.' She refused to look at him.

Liz bustled in. 'To be honest with you, I needed to get away from Bridget for a bit. You know what I mean?'

Josie wasn't sure if she should nod or not, but it didn't matter. Liz, with a roll of her eyes, took Josie's agreement for granted. Josie blinked when Liz pulled out a casserole from her basket and popped it in the oven.

'I told Bridge I was eating out tonight. I hope you don't mind.'

Josie shook her head. 'Not at all.'

Liz settled herself in Clancy's camp chair. 'No offence, Kent, but my Hungarian beef stew is a whole lot tastier than your tinned soup.'

Kent straddled one of the hard chairs. 'None taken.'

As the rich aroma of the casserole filled the air, Josie's mouth started to water. From the furtive glances Kent sent towards the oven, she guessed his did too.

'It'll be ready in thirty to forty minutes.' Liz edged her chair closer to the bed. 'Just long enough for us to have a cosy, girly chat.'

Kent shot to his feet. 'I'll, umm, go do some stuff.'

Josie couldn't mistake the wistful glance he directed towards them, though. She remembered Clancy's comment the day of the fête, about how Kent wasn't cut out for all this solitude. She wanted to ask him what stuff he had to do.

She wanted to ask him to stay.

Then she remembered she was a millstone around his neck. It wasn't company he pined for. At least, not hers. It'd be the food. And it smelt so good she didn't blame him.

'I'll be serving up in forty minutes, so if you don't want to miss out…'

Kent grinned and it did the strangest things to Josie's insides. A grin like that should come with warning bells and flashing lights so a person had the chance to look away before it bammed them right between the eyes. So they had a chance to maintain at least a scrap of balance.

'I'll be back.' He settled his hat on his head, touched the brim in a farewell salute and swaggered out.

Josie couldn't help but admire the view as he left.

Liz leaned forward and touched Josie's arm. Josie could see the strain on her face. 'This is going to sound awful, but your getting sick is a godsend to me. Don't take it the wrong way, love.' She patted Josie's hand. 'I'm sorry you're feeling poorly.'

Josie didn't doubt it.

'But it does give me an excuse to get out of the house.'

Josie sat up a little straighter. 'Is it really that bad?'

Liz nodded. 'Your having breakfast with us helped me cope with her. Deflected her attention from me for a bit. She makes me feel like an invalid.' She paused. 'I loved Ted and I miss him terribly, but just because he's no longer here doesn't mean I can't look after myself.'

'Of course not.'

'But you try telling Bridge that.'

Bridget was pretty overbearing. 'She means well.'

'Oh, I know that, love. If she didn't I'd have turfed her out on her ear by now. But coming to see you not only gives me a break from her, but also makes me feel useful again.' She hitched herself up. 'I'm not ready to be put out to pasture just yet.'

Josie's throat started to thicken.

'I finally have a reason to cook dinner again if you know what I mean.'

Josie knew exactly what she meant. For the first week after her father had died, she hadn't seen much point in cooking for one. She hadn't felt much like eating either.

'So if you don't mind, I'd like to stretch your illness out for at least a week. Then I'll have to think of something else because I honestly don't know what I'm going to do once you leave.'

Josie gulped. A lie of omission was still a lie, and she couldn't do it. 'Liz, I might be going home as soon as tomorrow. I asked Kent,' insisted more like, 'to call my brothers to come and collect me.'

Liz stiffened. 'Get him to call them back and say you've changed your mind. You don't really want to cut your holiday short, do you?'

'I… But…I can't keep being such a burden on Kent.'

'Nonsense. You're good for him.'

She was? How?

Before she could ask, Liz had rushed on. 'How are you a burden? The worst is past. Kent doesn't need to sit up with you all night now, and you'll be right as rain after a bit of bed rest. What does he have to do? I'll cook you dinner in the evening and,' she folded her arms, 'I know how much Clancy is looking forward to taking care of your lunch. He dropped by the store as pleased as punch about it.'

Josie bit her lip.

'All Kent has to do is make you a piece of toast in the mornings and pop his head around the door a couple of times a day to check if you need anything.'

When it was put like that…

'In fact, he'll be gaining from the arrangement because he can have his dinner with us instead of cooking it for himself.'

That was true.

'And I need you to help me figure out what I'm going to do about Bridge.' Liz leaned across and clasped Josie's hand. 'Please?'

A great yearning opened up inside her. 'Well…if it's OK with Kent.'

Liz sat back and beamed. 'It'll be OK with Kent.'

'What'll be OK with me?' Kent said, sauntering into the cabin and pulling off his hat.

'If Josie changes her mind and stays on here after all.'

He swung around. 'Have you changed your mind?'

She nodded, unable for the moment to speak. But she

kept her gaze on his face. She couldn't have watched him any closer if she'd put him under a microscope, but no scowls, not even a fraction of a frown, appeared. His eyes didn't narrow, his shoulders didn't freeze into place and his mouth didn't tighten. In fact, he literally beamed at her.

'It's more than OK. It's great.'

It was?

'That is smelling seriously good.' He nodded towards the oven. 'How long—?'

'Long enough for you to go ring Josie's brothers and tell them she's staying on after all.'

'No problem.'

With a nod and a grin he left, and Josie found she couldn't work Kent Black out at all. 'The tennis club,' she said, dragging her attention back to Liz. At least Liz made sense. 'Bridget needs something else to organise other than you. Does she like tennis?'

'Yes!' The word whistled out between Kent's teeth as he strode up to the house. He wanted to punch the air in victory. Josie was staying.

Not for good, he reminded himself. Just until the end of next week, but long enough for him to get her well and strong again. He wanted to celebrate. He pulled open the fridge and seized the neck of a bottle of chardonnay then remembered Josie couldn't drink while taking medication. He pushed it back in and pulled out several cans of lemonade instead. They'd celebrate properly when she was well.

Not him and Josie on their own, though. No. An image of candlelight and champagne and Josie in those cute little PJs of hers and—

He went tight and hard, his thickness straining against the denim of his jeans. He bit back an oath and tried to replace the image with a different one—he, Liz and Clancy holding a little party to send Josie off. That could be fun.

Not as fun as the first image, though.

He pulled his mind back, seized the phone and punched in Marty's business number. 'This is Kent Black,' he barked at the answering machine. 'Josie will be staying till the end of next week as planned.' Then he hung up.

He hadn't told Liz about his conversation with Marty, just that Josie had asked him to contact her brothers to come and collect her. The depth of Liz and Clancy's horror at the idea had surprised him. They'd done a sterling job at convincing her to stay, at convincing her she was needed. At convincing her she was no trouble at all. He'd never have managed that on his own.

And the way they'd marched into her cabin with its bright splashes of colour and its easy laughter, its comforting cosiness…all at ease and with that lazy kind of energy that spoke of goodwill and friendship, had made him realise everything his own life lacked. It gave him a glimpse of what life with a woman like Josie would be like.

Liz and Clancy would miss her when she left.

There was no denying it: so would he. But a man like him had no right messing with a woman like Josie.

He pushed that thought away and seized the lemonades. It was time to go and enjoy dinner with Josie. And Liz; he hadn't forgotten Liz.

When Liz left, Kent tidied up. He thought Josie had dozed off, but when he turned he found her watching him. He rolled his shoulders, shifted his weight from the balls of his feet to his heels and back again. He wondered if she sensed his reluctance to leave the cosiness of her cabin. 'Not tired?'

'I feel pleasantly lazy. I'm glad you wouldn't let me help clean up.'

Her honesty made him grin, put him at ease.

She readjusted a pillow at her back. 'Tell me about your sister.'

It took a moment for the words to hit him, and when they did they stabbed through him with a ferocity that took his breath. He took a step back and went to shout an unthinking 'No!' but clamped down on his lips until he'd brought the impulse under control. The night was cool but that didn't account for the coldness that rushed through him. 'Why?' The word sounded sharp in the silence of the cabin but Josie seemed oblivious to his reaction, to the difficulty he had breathing.

'Because I always wanted a sister.'

He thought of her brothers, took in her wistful expression, and understood why.

'What was her name? What things did she like to do?'

For Josie's sake he tried to think past the pain. 'Her name was Rebecca. I always called her Beck. Everyone else called her Becky.' His words came out short and halting as a picture of Beck's face turning to laugh at him in her sailing boat rose in his mind.

'I've always liked that name.' She shaded her eyes against the brightness of the overhead light. 'Would it be OK if we turned on the lamp?'

He switched on the lamp, turned off the overhead light and a warm glow suffused the room. Josie patted the bed beside her, her lips curved in a soft smile he wanted to fall into. He sat in Clancy's camp chair instead. He couldn't trust himself any closer to her than that. Not when the dark beat at the windows, not when this room and this woman transported him away from his lonely mountain. If he was fanciful he'd say Josie's cabin was an Aladdin's cave where fairy tales came true.

Only he was too old to believe in fairy tales.

'Was Becky a girly girl or a tomboy?'

That made him laugh. 'In company butter wouldn't melt in her mouth. But when nobody was watching she'd try and out-rough and out-tumble me.'

Josie grinned. 'Did she succeed?'

'Not a chance.' He grinned too. 'She was two years younger and not much bigger than you.'

'What did she like to do?'

He told her about Beck's love of sailing, the job she'd had as a pathologist, her addiction to candied ginger, and about the time when she was fifteen and she'd dyed her hair such a deep purple they'd spent an entire Christmas calling her Miss Plum. And the more he talked the easier it became. Finally he stopped and he couldn't have said why, but he felt lighter.

'I envy you,' Josie sighed. 'Not losing Becky, of course. That's awful.'

Sadness swept through him, but the weight didn't press back down.

'But the relationship the two of you had... It was really lovely.'

He nodded. He'd been in danger of forgetting. He eyed Josie for a moment. 'It's not like that with you and your brothers?'

He waited for her to tense up, but she didn't. 'They're

over ten years older than me. We didn't grow up together. They're the children of my father's first marriage.'

A wealth of meaning emerged from her words. Kent suddenly saw the picture clearly—along with what he suspected was Marty and Frank's resentment and jealousy of their younger half-sibling.

'Their lives have been harder than mine,' she added as if she read his mind. 'They grew up with their mother and she was a bitter woman, hard.'

'That's not your fault,' he pointed out gently.

'No, but I want to build whatever bridges with them that I can. I promised my father I'd try.' She fixed him with a look. 'What did Marty say when you spoke to him?'

'I left a message on his answering machine,' he hedged.

'Not tonight, but earlier when you spoke to him.'

He didn't want her upset, but he didn't want to lie to her either. He wanted her on her guard around this Marty and Frank. 'He said he was snowed under with work and would find it difficult to get away before next Tuesday.'

'Oh.'

At the look on her face he wanted to smash Marty all over again.

'They're always so busy,' she sighed. 'I think they hide behind their work.' She pleated the blanket between her fingers. 'I think they're afraid to love me.'

'What kind of nonsense is that?' he exploded.

She met his gaze head-on. 'I'd say it was your kind of nonsense, Kent.'

He shot to his feet, rubbed the back of his nape. 'It's getting late. It's time you got some rest.'

'Scaredy cat,' she murmured, but she settled back without demur as he pulled the covers up around her shoulders.

'Goodnight, Josie.'

'Goodnight, Kent.'

He hovered for a moment, wanting to kiss her forehead, but he pulled back at the last moment. Her taunt followed him all the way back to the house and plagued his sleep like a stray dog that fed on his dreams.

On Friday afternoon after Clancy left, Josie finally grew sick of staring at four walls. Actually, she'd grown sick of it yesterday, but today her inactivity really started to pall. This morning she'd argued with Kent about exchanging her pyjamas for real clothes, and lost. Pulling her wrap more firmly about her and tying it at her waist, Josie folded the camp chair, took it out to the veranda, unfolded it again and collapsed into it, breathing hard. She hated how the smallest thing wore her out.

She'd hated arguing with Kent too.

She cringed when she remembered the things she'd shouted at him. She'd called him a tyrant. And a voyeur. She still couldn't believe she'd said that.

He'd laughed at her, and she'd wanted to stamp her feet—a near impossible feat when confined to bed.

She doubted he even saw her as a woman now. She scowled. Oh, yes, he gave her friendly concern, teasingly derided her chess skills and praised the excellence of her crossword-solving skills.

She knew she was sinking low when she clung to praise about crosswords.

Somehow he'd purged his desire for her and she wanted to know how. Though maybe he hadn't had all that much to begin with. Her scowl deepened. She just wasn't his kind of woman, was she? That new sense of closeness that had developed between them since they'd talked about their siblings had disappeared too. In some imperceptible way Kent was withdrawing from her. And she didn't know how to stop him.

She made an impatient noise in the back of her throat. She hadn't come on this holiday to obsess about a man. If he wanted to withdraw that was his business. She'd come to formulate a plan for the rest of her life, remember? She was no closer to doing that than when she'd arrived.

And she only had a week left. Marty and Frank would be expecting an answer to that particular question at the end of all this. She could practically see their serious half-frowns, hear their foot-tapping impatience.

Oh, for heaven's sake! What business was it of theirs? It was not as if they had to financially support her or...

They were her brothers. She chided herself for her lack of charity. Of course they worried about her. And now that her father was gone she hoped they might forge closer ties.

She scowled again. She was all for promoting closer ties, but they needn't think they could bully her.

'Heck! Whose blood are you after?'

Josie started then drooled. Kent. She swiped a hand across her chin.

'Still imagining skinning me alive after our spat this morning?'

His grin told her he didn't harbour any hard feelings and she found herself smiling back at him. 'No, though I find myself cringing every time I remember calling you a voyeur.'

He eased himself down onto the single step, his grin widening. 'Nah, don't feel bad about that. You've got me pegged. I'm waiting with bated breath for those cute little shortie pyjamas to make a comeback. Those fluffy sheep did strange things to me.'

His teasing fired the blood through her veins, although she knew he didn't mean it. 'Funny things?' She tried to ignore the burn of desire. 'Like falling all over the place laughing, right?'

'More like getting me hot and bothered when I imagine peeling them off your body.'

Josie gulped and the blood pumped through her so hard and hot she thought her fever had returned. Kent jerked back as if he couldn't believe he'd uttered the words. And just like that the tension coiled around them.

With a muttered curse, he leapt up and strode several feet away. Josie expected him to plunge straight into the cover of the trees and keep walking. Without a backward glance. When he didn't, her eyes, greedy for the sight of him, memorised every hard, lean angle of his body.

He always wore jeans and either a T-shirt or a long-sleeved chambray shirt, and she couldn't decide which did him the greater justice. The jeans, whether low-slung, stretch or bootleg, did strange things to her pulse. They also left her in little doubt of his, uh, assets.

And she literally drooled at the sight of thin cotton stretched across his shoulders and arms in those fitted T-shirts. But the faded blue chambray intensified the blue of his eyes and caught her up in fantasies of making love with him on long, lazy summer afternoons.

Oh, who was she kidding? It didn't matter what he wore for her to get caught up in those kinds of fantasies.

He swung back to face her and she could see him trying to fight a scowl. 'Sorry.' The word snapped out of him. 'You'd better forget I said that.'

She didn't want to forget. She wanted—

'We already decided that wouldn't be sensible.'

Had they? When? 'I'm tired of sensible,' she muttered.

His eyes darkened, then he grinned. 'Either way, Josephine Peterson, you're not physically up for an athletic bout of lovemaking. Besides, it's against doctor's orders.'

She knew he was right. If a shower wore her out, then how on earth…?

Pictures rose in her mind. Pictures that didn't help. She tried to push them away, far far away where they couldn't torment her.

'So, in the meantime,' he took his seat on the step again, 'why don't you tell me why you were glaring at this glorious view as if you meant to do it physical harm?'

CHAPTER NINE

JOSIE'S lips turned down and her shoulders sagged. Kent wanted to haul her into his lap, tuck her head under his chin and wrap his arms around her slight body until she stopped looking so glum.

Not a good idea.

He didn't do hugs. And he had no doubt that if he hugged Josie she'd get the wrong idea. He couldn't let that happen, couldn't let her rely on him in the long term.

A scowl shrugged through him. He shouldn't let her rely on him in the short term either.

If it wasn't for her darn brothers he wouldn't, but she needed someone to look out for her. She'd drawn the short straw in him, though maybe Clancy and Liz made up for it.

'Did Marty say anything else when you spoke to him? Has Frank called at all?'

Was she upset because of her brothers?

'Nope and nope.' He kept the snarl out of his voice. Just.

Her lips turned down more. 'I mean,' he added quickly, 'he was concerned about your health, of course. Relieved when I told him you'd be OK.' Because then he wouldn't be dragged away from his *oh-so-important work*.

Not that he'd rung in the last couple of days to check

on how she was doing. That knowledge hung in the silence between them. 'Why?'

She lifted one shoulder. 'No reason.'

'Are they why you looked fit to kill someone?' He understood that. In fact, he'd help her if she wanted.

'Oh, no.' She quickly shook her head and all the browns and russets and maples of her hair swished about her face before settling back around her shoulders. He wanted to reach out and touch it. He wanted to bury his face in it.

'But, you see, I haven't worked out what I'm going to do with the rest of my life yet and that's the reason for this holiday in the first place.'

The note of panic in her words hauled him back. He skewed around on the step to face her more fully. 'Let's back up a bit. Why can't you keep doing whatever it was you did before you came to Eagle Reach?' Had she been sacked or something?

She smiled, a sad smile that speared right through the centre of him. 'For the last two years I looked after my father. That job doesn't exist any more.'

Bile rose in his throat. 'I'm sorry I—'

'It's not your fault.' She waved his apology away. 'My father had dementia and I didn't want to place him in a nursing home so I completed an Assistant in Nursing course. I don't regret it. I cherish the time I spent with him.'

'But you don't want to do that any more?'

'No, I don't want to do that any more.' A shadow passed across her face. 'No. No more.'

He understood. Watching someone die was the hardest thing in the world. Especially when it was someone you loved.

'What did you do, Kent? Before your sea change and you came out here?'

The question caught him off guard. He'd known she hadn't believed him when he'd said it before. He hadn't bothered trying to set her straight and now it reeked of deceit. He rubbed the back of his neck.

'Kent?'

'I was a doctor.' Dedicated to saving people's lives. He'd removed himself from society pretty quick-smart once he realised he had a greater talent for destruction, though.

If he had an ounce of decency in him he'd leave Josie alone too.

'You're a doctor?' Josie shot forward so quickly she'd have fallen out of her chair if Kent hadn't reached out and steadied her. His fingers wrapped around her arm, warm and vibrant. More than anything, she wanted to fall into him. He removed his hand before she could do anything so stupid.

His close-lipped silence spoke volumes. 'I was a GP.'

It shouldn't have made sense, but in a strange way it did. She wanted to cry. 'And why—?'

She gulped back her words at his glare.

'I found I was unsuited to the profession.'

She didn't believe that for a moment. She refused to risk another soul-crushing glare by saying so, though. 'So, the doctor's orders I've been following have been yours?'

'Yes.'

It explained his professional detachment.

A wave of dizziness shook her. He hadn't stopped practising because of his mother and sister, had he?

'You're free to consult a second opinion, of course. Dr Jenkins does house calls. If you want I'll ring him and—'

'No.' She stared at him, horrified. 'I trust your judgement.' The scowl left his face but not his eyes. 'You made Molly well again, didn't you?'

At her name, Molly lifted her head and thumped her tail. She'd hardly left Josie's side since she'd been let back in after the worst of her illness had passed.

'And she was in way worse shape than me.'

His lips twisted into the wryest of smiles. 'I hate to point this out to you, Josie, but Molly is just a dog.'

'Molly isn't *just* anything. She's lovely and you made her well again, like you're making me well again. I don't think you're unsuited to the profession at all.' But she didn't want him to start scowling again so she didn't pursue that line further. She collapsed against the back of her chair. 'Not that it's doing me much good.'

His eyebrows shot up and she laughed, realising what she'd just said. 'I meant inspiration-wise. It won't help me sort out what to do with the rest of my life.' Marty and Frank's faces rose in front of her and her quick surge of humour evaporated in a puff that berated her for her frivolity.

One week. She glanced out at the view spread before her and couldn't hold back a sigh. Her eyes drifted to the man seated on the step.

'What did you do before you took on the care of your father?'

'I was halfway through a teaching degree.' He raised an eyebrow but she shook her head. 'The thought of study doesn't fill me with a great deal of enthusiasm. Besides, I don't want to leave Buchanan's Point and there aren't many opportunities for teachers in the local area.' It'd take years before she was posted there.

'Why don't you want to leave?'

'It's home.' It was that simple. 'It's where I belong. And then there's the house. It's been in the family for generations. I couldn't just leave it.'

'Couldn't your brothers look after it?'

Marty and Frank again. The sky became a little greyer, although there wasn't a cloud in it. 'The house belonged to my mother. Her family have lived in it since it was built over a hundred years ago.' And she wasn't selling it.

Kent stared at her for a moment then grinned as if eminently satisfied with something. 'If you've a house, Josie, then at least you've a roof over your head.'

'I have a home,' she corrected, which was more than Kent could boast out here at Eagle Reach, for all his cows and cabins.

His eyes gentled. 'Tell me about it.'

She shrugged. Where to start? But as she imagined her home her lips curved into a smile. 'It's beautiful. It's called Geraldine's Gardens and it's the only house on the bluff and it looks out over the town and beach. A little path winds down to a private beach. It's only tiny, but it is lovely.'

He sat up straighter. 'And the house?'

'It's beautiful too. Federation style, return verandas, fancy fretwork.' All of which took an enormous amount of upkeep. 'It is a little large for one person,' she admitted, 'but...but who knows what'll happen down the track?' She hoped to fill it with a family of her own one day.

'Too big?' His eyes narrowed. 'How many bedrooms?'

She hesitated. 'Eight.'

'Eight!' Kent shot to his feet. 'I...'

'Yeah, it's big.' And it took a lot of cleaning, but it was worth it. And she wasn't selling.

'Josie?'

She pulled her thoughts back. 'Hmm?'

'Marty and Frank are OK about the house?'

'Oh, no, they want me to sell it. They think it's too much for me.'

Kent's eyebrows knitted together.

'But the house is like a family heirloom.' She smiled up at him. Instinctively, she knew he'd understand. 'I need to preserve it to pass on to the next generation.'

He brushed the backs of his fingers across her cheek. 'I envy you your home, Josephine Peterson.'

Her heart thumped like a mad thing. 'Then you should come and visit some time. It's not like I don't have the room or anything. Next time you're passing through…' A pipedream, she knew. She also knew she was babbling.

He pulled his fingers back abruptly. 'Time you were back in bed.'

'But I'm not doing anything. I'm just sitting.'

Her argument died in her throat when he leaned down and picked her up. Her heart pounded so hard she swore there'd be bruises. 'I, umm…' Her tongue stuck to the roof of her mouth. She tried to unglue it. 'I can walk, you know?'

Not that she wanted to. She wanted to stay right here. She looped an arm around his shoulders, his broad, beautiful shoulders, and bit back a purr of pure pleasure.

His gaze met hers then flicked to her lips. She gulped. An insistent throb started up low, deep down in her abdomen. His lips opened and her breath stilled. Then he waggled those wicked eyebrows. 'I want you to conserve your energy. Doctor's orders.'

He made no move towards the door of the cabin, though. His hot male scent filled her nostrils, his hard body imprinted itself on hers and her heart continued to beat itself to a pulp.

'I, umm...' She wished she could speak properly. She gave a shaky laugh. 'I think I'd conserve a whole lot more energy if you put me down again.'

He grinned. 'Yeah?'

She loved his teasing. 'You do seriously wicked things to my pulse rate, Kent Black.'

He shook his head, mock serious. 'That's not good for conserving energy. You'll need to do something about that.'

Like what? All the images, ideas, suggestions flooding through her involved her expending a whole lot more energy, not conserving it. 'Doctor's orders, huh?'

'You bet.'

She trailed her fingers into the V of his shirt. Heat came off him in thick, drugging waves and she tugged gently at the hair there, revelling in its springiness, before tracing her hand back up his neck to his jaw. His breath caught when she ran her palm across the roughness of his half-day growth and hers quickened. The scrape of desire sparked from her palm to curl her toes.

His eyes turned a deep, dark navy. 'Josie.'

The single word growled out of his throat, but he made no move to set her down and a reckless triumph seized her. 'You know what?' She traced his lips with her fingers. 'I'm afraid of stray dogs and goannas and of the kind of solitude that means you don't clap eyes on another human being for three days straight, but I'm not afraid of this.'

She reached up and replaced her fingers with her lips. Kent's arms tightened around her and her whole body sang, but he held himself rigid, his lips refusing to respond as hers moved tentatively over his.

She'd never taken the initiative before. It part-appalled, part-thrilled her.

No, it wholly thrilled her. But Kent's lack of involvement sent a shock wave of frustration through her. Determination welled up, determination to draw out that response.

She traced the length of his bottom lip with her tongue, from left to right, slowly, savouring his taste and texture. 'Yum,' she murmured against the corner of his mouth when she reached it. Then she slipped her tongue inside to trace his inner lips, from right to left, and Kent jerked as if electrified.

Then he crushed her against him and his mouth devoured hers and she'd never known that so much feeling could go into a single kiss. She flung both her arms around his neck and kissed him back with everything inside her, a fury of need pulsing through her veins as his tongue teased and tangled with hers.

Both his arms went around her waist and the lower half of her body slid down his until the tips of her toes touched the ground. Pulled flush against him, the most sensitive part of her pressed against the hard length straining through the denim of his jeans, teasing her until nothing made sense except her overwhelming need for him. With an inarticulate moan, her head dropped back and Josie lost herself in sensation.

Kent branded her neck with kisses. One hand curved around her bottom to keep her planted hard up against him, the other tangled in the hair at her nape to draw her mouth back to his. He claimed drugging kiss after drugging kiss until she was a trembling, sobbing mass of need.

Then a fit of coughing claimed her.

She leaned against him after it finished, trying to get her

breath back, trying to draw strength into limbs that shook. His hands curved around her shoulders, steadying her, supporting her, but she sensed his withdrawal. Still…

What a kiss! She couldn't curb the exhilaration coursing through her body.

She wondered how soon they could do that again.

One look at Kent's face told her there'd be no repeat performances today. And from the look of that scowl, probably not tomorrow either.

Oh, well. It'd give her a chance to get her strength back. With a sigh of regret she pushed away from him. 'Well,' she started brightly, 'that was…'

The words died in her throat for the second time when he swept her up in his arms and strode inside with her. Being held by Kent felt like coming home.

And she was homesick. Big time.

His face might be grim, but he laid her on the bed with a gentleness normally reserved for priceless artworks. She blinked furiously when he took a hasty step away, bit back a moan of loss.

He glared as she nestled down against the pillows. 'That was—'

'Heavenly,' she announced. 'When can we do it again?'

His jaw dropped then he swung away and stalked straight back out of the cabin.

'Kent Black,' she murmured, her eyes fluttering closed. 'You are one sexy man.'

She wondered if he'd ever stop running.

'Checkmate.'

Josie pushed the chessboard away with a sigh. 'I'm not improving.'

'You don't concentrate,' Kent chided.

How on earth was a girl supposed to concentrate when Kent's lips hovered just there across the chessboard and created all kinds of tempting fantasies inside her, huh?

Fantasies that were way more exciting than beating him at chess.

It was Sunday. Two whole days since their kiss. But for the past two days that kiss was all Josie could think about. She'd completed her three days of prescribed bed rest, but she could tell Kent didn't think her recovered enough for more kissing.

'What about catering?'

His words momentarily dragged her away from thoughts of kissing. 'Umm…' What had she missed?

'You could start up your own catering company.'

Oh, they were back to that. Still, it was better than nothing, she supposed. She'd expected him to bolt out of here as soon as he'd annihilated her at chess. As he had yesterday. As if afraid she'd try and kiss him again.

She wasn't going to kiss him again until she'd recovered her full strength. She had no intention of letting a little cough get in her way next time.

'I can't go into catering.' She'd already considered the idea and dismissed it.

'Why not?'

'Suzanna de Freits has the market cornered in Buchanan's Point, not to mention the surrounding seaside villages of Crescent Beach and Diamond Head.'

'Afraid of a little competition?'

She grinned at the rallying note in his voice. He obviously thought she needed a pep talk. 'Her savouries are better than mine.'

'I bet her chocolate cake doesn't come close.'

Bless his heart. He actually looked as if he meant that. Thoughts of kissing rose up through her again. She shook her head. 'Suzanna is a single mother of three school-age children.' And a friend. 'She works hard. I'm not poaching her customers.'

'Not even to save your house...home?'

'People are more important than bricks and mortar.' Even when those bricks and mortar made up Geraldine's Gardens. 'I'd rather take on another dementia patient than do that.' Maybe it wouldn't be so bad if she wasn't nursing her father? Her stomach curdled at the thought all the same.

'Don't do that.'

She may not have any choice. Frustration shot through her. She should've spent the last two days searching for a solution to this particular problem rather than obsessing about kissing Kent.

'Ooh, humungous huntsman.' She shrank in her chair and pointed to the kitchen wall.

With an exaggerated sigh, Kent climbed to his feet, rolled up yesterday's newspaper and advanced on the hapless spider. Josie scampered after him and snatched the paper out of his hands. 'What do you think you're doing?'

He stared at her. 'I'm going to squash it.'

Her eyes widened. 'But you're like a hundred million times bigger than it.' She whacked him on the arm with the rolled-up newspaper. 'It's only a spider.'

'You were the one that said—'

'I didn't say kill it!' She whacked him again. 'And just because I'm female doesn't mean I run yelling and screaming from a spider.'

'You do from dogs and goannas.'

'I'm going to pretend I didn't hear that.' She glared at him. 'Out of my way.'

Josie unrolled the newspaper, folded it in half then eased in under the spider's legs—slowly, slowly—until the spider sat on the end of the newspaper. Without taking her eyes off it, she walked across the room and outside.

She was halfway between her cabin and the nearest stand of trees when the spider rose up on all of its eight legs and raced the length of the newspaper towards her. She dropped the newspaper with a squeal and jumped back.

Kent laughed so hard from his vantage point on the veranda he had to sit down. 'I didn't say I wanted it on me!'

She glared at him, but he only laughed harder. 'I've found your new career, Josie.'

'This should be good,' she muttered, but her lips started to twitch.

'Stand-up comedy.'

'Oh, ha-ha, very funny.' She rolled her eyes and collapsed onto the veranda beside him. Then glanced around warily. 'Where did it go?'

'Not scared of spiders, huh?'

She lifted her chin. 'Not scared enough to kill them.'

He grinned down at her, shook his head, went to turn away then swung back and kissed her, hard. Once.

Her eyes glazed over. When they finally cleared she could see him already regretting the impulsive act.

'Wow!' She swore she'd keep it light if it was the last thing she did. 'With that kind of positive reinforcement I'll never be afraid of spiders again. Though,' some imp made her add, 'I'll need another two or three sessions of that same therapy before I'm fully cured.'

His grin, when it came, was one of those long, slow,

crooked ones that made her heart go boom. Desire slowly burned through her.

'You're impossible, you know that?'

She shrugged. 'If stand-up comedy is my thing then I'd best get in some practice.' But the stand-up comedy thing was just a joke. They both knew that. Her smile dipped as her original problem bore down on her again.

Kent nudged her shoulder. 'Earth to Josie.'

She shook herself. 'What are you up to for the next hour or so?'

His eyes narrowed. 'Why?'

She leaned back and raised an eyebrow. 'You know, that question just begs for a suggestive comeback.' She took pity on him when he dragged a hand down his face. 'I feel like making chocolate cake.'

She went to jump up but his hand on her arm stopped her. 'You're supposed to be taking it easy.'

'Don't worry.' She shot him a cheeky grin. 'You'll be the one doing all the hard work.'

Kent didn't know how Josie managed it, but she made baking a cake fun. He'd tried to tell himself he'd only hung around to prevent her from overdoing it, but that was a lie. He'd stayed because he couldn't stay away. In fact, if he could've eased her suffering and his own worry, Josie's illness was probably the highlight of the last year.

He cut that thought off, angry with himself. But then Josie smiled and the tightness inside him eased. He enjoyed watching her deft hands measuring out ingredients. He enjoyed her teasing his ineptness with a wooden spoon. He enjoyed watching the colour bloom back into her cheeks.

Josie popped the cake in the oven then swiped a finger

along the inside rim of the mixing bowl, gathering as much cake mix as she could, then popped the finger in her mouth and closed her eyes in bliss. He enjoyed that too.

'Yum.' As if aware of his gaze she opened her eyes and held out the wooden spoon for him. 'Go on,' she urged when he hesitated. 'I bet you and Becky fought over the wooden spoon when you were kids and your mum baked a cake.'

He jerked back, waiting for acid to fill his stomach at the mention of his family. It didn't come, so he reached for the spoon. 'She wasn't much of a one for baking cakes. Soup was her thing.' Big, rich pots of simmering goodness. In winter he'd rush home from school, his mouth watering with the knowledge of what awaited him when he got there.

He hadn't thought of that in a long time.

'Soup.' Josie stared at him in mock indignation. 'Your mum cooked the most scrumptious homemade soup ever, and don't tell me she didn't because I can tell from the expression on your face that she did. Yet you had the gall to feed me tinned stuff?'

He grinned, but he wished he had cooked her up a big pot of soup. 'To be honest, I didn't think you'd much notice…or care.'

'To be honest,' she leaned in close as if confiding a secret, 'you'd be right.'

He wanted to kiss her again, so he retreated to the table and set about licking the spoon clean. Josie had made this cabin the cosiest darn place on this side of the mountain. On second thoughts, probably the cosiest place on the whole mountain. He'd never set foot inside Smiley McDonald's house, but he'd bet Mrs Smiley McDonald didn't have the same knack Josie did. The knack of creating a home from nothing.

It'd started him thinking too. He could make improvements to all these cabins. The way Josie had done. And up at the house too. His mind fizzed with new possibilities.

Maybe she should go into interior decorating. He wondered if a person needed qualifications or whether they—

He jerked in his seat as the solution to Josie's problem slapped him on the head. 'How many bedrooms did you say you had at Geraldine's Gardens?'

'Eight.' She didn't turn from washing the dishes.

'And how many living areas?'

She tossed a glance over her shoulder then shrugged and went back to the dishes. 'There's the formal and informal lounge rooms, the family room, the sunroom, the breakfast room and the library. Oh, and there's a ballroom.'

How big was this place? 'Josie,' he tried to keep his tone measured, tried to keep the excitement out of his voice, 'why don't you turn Geraldine's Gardens into a bed and breakfast?'

She dropped the bowl she was washing and swung to face him. Soapsuds dripped to her bare toes. Her mouth formed a perfect O and Kent found himself wanting to kiss it.

Again.

Josie couldn't contain her excitement. She raced over to the table, plonked herself down and gripped his hands. 'Do you really think I could do that?'

'Sure you could.'

He squeezed her hands before gently detaching them and leaning back to survey her. She wanted to wriggle beneath his scrutiny, but she didn't. She stared back, held her breath and hoped he liked what he saw.

'I mean, look at what you've done with this place.'

She knew her grin must be ridiculously wide. Kent had the kind of rugged good looks that could make her pulse perform a tango, but it was more than that. He possessed a kindness, a generosity, and, no matter how hard he tried to hide it, it always seemed to find a way to the surface.

She knew now what Clancy meant. Kent didn't suit this solitude any more than she did. Burying himself out here like this was a crime.

And none of your business, a voice intoned inside her.

Pooh. What did she care about that? She'd poke her nose in where it wasn't wanted if she thought it'd do any good. But it wouldn't. Kent wouldn't listen to her. He'd scowl and become a stranger and be glad to see the back of her.

'If you can manage all this here,' he continued, 'how much more could you achieve at Geraldine's Gardens?'

Excitement shifted through her.

'I bet there are plenty of local handicrafts in Buchanan's Point you could feature.'

She could theme the rooms. And she could get in tourist brochures for areas of local interest. Maybe even arrange the odd tour or two to the near by vineyards or the recreated colonial town less than an hour away.

'And you could showcase local produce.'

Ooh, yes. Suzanna made the most fabulous preserved fruit, and someone from the women's institute would be happy to provide her with pickles and jam.

Kent leaned forward. 'More to the point, you're great with people, Josie. You'd make a wonderful hostess.'

She found herself starting to choke up…then she sat back, her shoulders sagging. 'There are hundreds of little seaside towns all along the coast of New South Wales identical to Buchanan's Point. Not to mention the larger centres that offer nightlife and restaurants and attractions galore. How on earth do I compete with them? What can I offer except a stay in a lovely house?'

'You need a selling point.' Kent drummed his fingers against the table. 'How much did you hate the nursing aspects of looking after your father?'

She gazed at him blankly.

'I mean the bathing and feeding, making sure he took his medication et cetera?'

'Oh, I didn't mind that at all.' It was the watching him die that she'd hated.

'Then why don't you tailor your b & b for invalids and their carers? There's a rapidly expanding aged population in this country. There's a market out there, Josie, just waiting to be tapped into. Your qualifications are an added bonus, especially if you can offer the carers a couple of hours' free time for themselves each day.'

Her jaw dropped. There'd been days when she'd have killed for a couple of hours off. Not for anything special, just a haircut or to browse in the local library, or even just to sit over a cup of coffee she hadn't made herself. It would've helped. Marty and Frank had always been too busy to sit with their father much. And she wouldn't have dreamed of asking anyone else except in an emergency.

'Have you any savings?'

'Some. Why?'

'Because you'll need something to tide you over until the money starts coming in.'

Good point. She did a quick calculation in her head. If she was frugal she'd have enough for a few months.

'Advertising will be your major expense.'

Oops, she hadn't factored that in. She wondered if the bank would give her a loan.

'Let me invest in the project, Josie.'

Her jaw dropped.

'Don't worry, I'm not being altruistic.' His grin said otherwise. 'I have plenty of money stashed away, and I have a feeling I'll be seeing quite a return on that money.'

Did he really have that much faith in her? The blue of his eyes held such an earnest appeal Josie almost said yes. She dragged her eyes from his and forced herself to think the idea through.

Her heart sank. She tried to swallow the bile that rose in her throat. 'No,' she croaked.

He sat back as if she'd struck him. 'Why not?'

Because he'd made it clear he wasn't interested in any kind of personal commitment. If he invested in her project he'd be hovering in the background of her life for heaven only knew how long, kissing her then running away. She wouldn't be able to stop herself from building larger-scale fantasies around him.

She'd never move on.

She stared at the rugged, lean lines of his face and her mouth went dry. Some time over the last three weeks she'd gone and done the stupidest thing in the world. She'd fallen in love with Kent Black.

When? While he nursed her through the worst of her fever? Or earlier…when he rescued her from the goanna, perhaps, or the first time they'd played chess? Maybe it was the day of the church fête, or the time she'd caught him skinny-dipping down at the river or—

Enough already!

He'd never love her back. Panic pounded through her.

She was afraid of dogs and goannas and ticks and spiders. She was even a bit afraid of Bridget Anderson. He could never love a woman who was like that.

Numbness settled over the surface of her skin. Even if by some miracle he grew fond of her, she could never live out here with him in all his isolation. It went against everything she was.

And he would never give it up.

Stalemate.

Kent leaned across the table, took her chin in his hand and studied her face closely. 'You're pale. You need to rest. We'll talk about this later.'

Josie wanted to laugh, not because she found it funny but because her heart was breaking and Kent's concern over a mere chest infection seemed suddenly trivial.

Nevertheless, she made no murmur of protest, but climbed onto the sofa bed and buried her face in a pillow.

The minutes seemed like hours as she waited for Kent to finish washing the last of the dishes, to dry them then take the cake out of the oven when the timer rang. She could've groaned out loud when he started tidying the cabin. She sensed him hovering over her, but she refused to turn around, refused to unbury her face from the pillow.

Only when she heard him tiptoe out did she let the hot tears slide down her cheeks.

CHAPTER TEN

'WHY won't you let me invest in your b & b?'

It was Monday afternoon and Clancy had just left. Since yesterday, she and Kent had circled around each other very carefully—with the emphasis on the very. Super-polite. Extremely wary.

Josie didn't know how she'd get through the next week if things remained like this. She didn't know how she'd get through it if they didn't. The one thing she did know—she didn't want to have this conversation.

Kent straddled one of the hard chairs and folded his arms along its back. They bulged in his fitted T-shirt, each muscle clearly delineated in pale blue cotton. Josie curled herself into a corner of the sofa and tried not to drool. She might not want to have this conversation, but she didn't want to stop ogling him either.

That probably made her a female chauvinist pig. She cleared her throat and dragged her gaze away from his tempting arms, his tempting lips. She doubted she could look at him and talk at the same time.

She hated confrontations. Wherever possible she avoided them. Kent's body language, though, told her she wasn't going to avoid this one. They could keep this pleasant and polite. She pulled in a breath. It didn't have to descend into an argument or a fight.

'Why are you refusing my money?'

'I really appreciate your offer, Kent, but I'm not going to risk your money when I don't know if I can pull this off.'

'You'll succeed. I know you will.'

His smile almost undid her. Of course they could keep this pleasant. They were adults, weren't they?

'If I invest in your project, I know I'll get a good return for my money.'

She couldn't let him go on thinking he could change her mind. 'What do you want with more money? It's not like you have anything to spend it on out here.'

His jaw dropped and she hated herself, but she ploughed on all the same. 'What kind of input would you expect to have at Geraldine's Gardens if you did invest, huh?'

'None. All the business decisions would be yours.'

He meant it too. She could see that. A lump lodged in her throat and refused to budge. 'I don't want your charity,' she finally managed.

He leaned forward. 'Where will you get the money for the initial outlay, then?'

At least she could answer that. She'd lain awake last night pondering that exact same question. She forced her smile to widen. 'From Marty and Frank. This is just the kind of project designed to bring us closer.'

They were family. They'd help. This scheme was perfect. She crossed her fingers and prayed she was right, because she had a feeling she'd need their support when she returned home. In more ways than one.

Kent leapt up, his chair crashing to the floor. 'Marty and Frank!'

She hunched her shoulders up around her ears. What on earth…? They were supposed to be keeping this pleasant.

'Are you mad?'

No, but he was. Hopping mad. And she didn't get it. 'They're family. They're who I should turn to.' And if it all went to plan it'd be perfect.

Perfect except Kent wouldn't be in her life.

He wouldn't be in her life if he did invest in her b & b anyway, not in the way she wanted, so it was a moot point.

It didn't feel like a moot point.

'Do you seriously think they'll help you?'

He stared at her the same way she'd stared at that tick as it had burrowed into her flesh. Her chin shot up, though her shoulders stayed hunched. 'Why wouldn't they?'

They would. Of course they would.

'They sent you out here, didn't they?'

'Which just goes to show how thoughtful and—'

'Garbage. It just goes to show how little they know you.'

She hated the thread of truth that wove its way through his words. She resisted it. Her brothers had sent her on this holiday because they knew she'd needed it.

'For Pete's sake,' he glared at her, 'this is your idea of the holiday from hell.'

Had been—past tense. She'd come back. To visit Clancy and Liz. She wouldn't stay at Eagle Reach, though. She had a feeling she wouldn't be welcome. 'It's turned out all right,' she argued.

'You got sick!'

'That could've happened anywhere.'

He swung away, raked his hands through his hair then swung back. 'You can't trust them.'

She gaped at him. She couldn't believe he'd just said

that, couldn't believe he'd try and dash all her hopes in one fell blow. They were the only hopes she had left.

She leapt up, trembling. 'You don't even know my brothers. You've spoken to Marty on the phone for all of two minutes and…'

A horrible thought struck her. 'Unless you haven't told me everything. Is there something I should know?'

What on earth could Marty have said to make Kent react like this? Her mouth went dry. For one craven moment she wished she could call that question back.

Kent stared at her. He rolled his shoulders then shoved his hands in his pockets and glanced away. 'No.'

Her shoulders sagged until her thoughts caught up with her relief. *You can't trust them!* 'Then…' Her mouth worked but for a moment no sound would come out. 'Then you're basing your assumption on what you know of me. You think they'll take advantage of me, because I can't look after myself. You think I can be manipulated just like that.' She took two steps forward and clicked her fingers under his nose. 'You don't think I have a backbone.' Which was why he would never love her.

'You won't get any arguments from me on that score.'

She swallowed back her sudden nausea and wished she'd never seen herself through his eyes. Frustration rose up and engulfed her in a red mist. She'd give him backbone! 'Where on earth do you get off, lecturing me about backbone when you're the one who's burying himself out here in the back of beyond like some scared kid?'

The silence that echoed in the room after her hasty words made her take a step back. Oh, dear lord. She gulped. Then she hitched up her chin and held her ground. In for a penny… 'I don't care how responsible you think you are for your mother's and sister's deaths. You weren't.'

'Don't you…'

He didn't finish the sentence. He shoved a finger under her nose instead, but she batted it away. 'You weren't the one who lit the match and torched the house. You're doing penance for a crime that's not yours.'

His head snapped back. 'It was my job to keep them safe.'

But even as his eyes blazed their fury, Josie saw the desolation in their depths. She had to bite her lip to keep from crying out.

'I should've known what he'd do.' The words wrenched out of him, harsh and merciless.

Josie wanted to cry. And she wanted to drag his head down to her shoulder and hold him. Neither would help, so she gulped back the impulses and glared at him. 'Why?' she demanded. 'Why should you be gifted as a mind-reader when the rest of us aren't? Why should you have known what he'd do when neither your mother nor sister guessed either?'

He blinked.

'I know you'd have saved them if you could've. I know you'd swap places with them if you could. But you can't.'

The lines around his mouth tightened, stark in the tanned lines of his face, then that colour too seemed to leach away, leaving him grey. Her heart ached so hard her knees threatened to buckle.

'You blame yourself and hide out here because it's easier than risking all and learning how to live again.' Anger flashed in his eyes but, curiously, she wasn't afraid of it. 'So until you're prepared to rejoin the land of the living, Kent Black, don't lecture me about backbone.'

Then she had to sit.

His lip curled. 'You can do what you damn well please, but don't tell me how to live my life.'

The anger in his eyes chilled over with the iciness of his withdrawal and Josie hated it. 'What? That's a right you reserve for yourself, is it?' She wanted him angry again. 'Trust me, Josie, but don't trust your brothers?'

If possible, his eyes became colder. She gave a shaky laugh. 'You know as well as I do you should be out there being a doctor and saving what lives you can. It's what you want to do, what you were born to do.'

She watched him close himself up, become the stranger she'd met on her first day here at Eagle Reach, and there wasn't anything she could do about it. She had no words left with which to reach him. Except childish words like 'Grow up', or 'Please love me'.

She couldn't tell him she loved him. He'd hate that worst of all. She glanced up and met his gaze. 'I'll accept your help for my b & b if you go back to being a doctor.'

The pulse at his jaw worked. 'No deal.'

Her heart slumped at his coldness. The last of her hope keeled over and died. She hadn't helped him at all. She'd just raked up painful memories and made him relive them.

He was right not to love her.

But before she could apologise, find some way to make amends, Kent spun around and stalked out of the cabin. Even though Josie recovered more of her strength every day, she knew she'd never keep up with him.

Molly whined and poked her head out from her hidey-hole behind the sofa. 'I screwed up, Molly,' Josie sighed. Molly crept out and rested her head on Josie's knee. 'Not only will he never love me, but he'll probably never speak to me again.'

So much for one final week of treasured memories. She had about as much hope of Kent kissing her again as she did of sprouting feathers and laying an egg.

Josie didn't see Kent for the rest of the day. Or the next. Or the day after that either. She and Molly took short forays down to the river, where Josie sat on the bank and lifted her face to the sun, but it never seemed to penetrate to the chill around her heart. She skimmed stones and prayed for a glimpse of Kent.

The stones sank. Kent stayed away.

She'd return in time to have lunch with Clancy. And a game of dominoes. She baked in the afternoons, or read. She did the crossword. Alone.

She ate dinner with Liz, and as soon as Liz left she climbed into bed and pulled the covers over her head.

Was this what the rest of her life entailed—missing Kent? She tried to harden herself to it. During the days it almost worked.

At night the pretence fell away.

She didn't notice the changing greens of the landscape any more, or the silver flash of the river. She didn't see the fat, ice-cream whiteness of the clouds in the bright blue of the sky. Each day dawned grey, no matter how hard the sun shone.

On Thursday she returned from her walk with Molly to find a note pinned to her door. She recognised Kent's strong, masculine scrawl and her stupid heart leapt. She snatched it up. Unfolded it.

'Jacob Pengilly rang. Asked if you'd return his call.'

That was it. No *Dear Josie*. No *Regards, Kent*. Nothing.

Her stupid heart kept leaping about in her chest though, because it knew that this was the perfect excuse to go and see him. Clutching the note, she set off towards his house. She didn't wait to pull in a breath before she knocked on his back screen door. She deliberately turned round to peer at the lush greenness of the forest beyond his back fence. Colour started to intrude itself on the periphery of her consciousness again.

She knew the exact moment he stood behind her because she could smell him. That unique combination of wood smoke and hot man. She closed her eyes and breathed him in before she turned. The screen door partially obscured him, thankfully. Her heart thump-thumped hard enough as it was.

'Hi.' She tried for a smile.

He didn't return her greeting.

She lifted the note. 'I got the message. Thank you.'

Still nothing. Not a word. Not even a flicker of recognition. Certainly no interest.

She blew a strand of hair out of her eyes. 'May I use your phone?'

She waited for him to tell her to go to blazes.

One…two…three fraught seconds went by. Just as she was about to give up and walk away, he pushed the screen door open. Josie, afraid he'd change his mind, squeezed past him in double-quick time then berated herself for not making more of it, for not slowing it down and relishing the brush of her breasts against his chest, her arm against his arm.

Kent, silent still, waved her towards the phone.

She made for it, stopped then spun back. 'Are you all right?' She marched back to peer up into his face. 'Are you sick or anything?'

'No, why?'

Because he was so darn silent, that was why. 'No reason.' She backed off towards the phone. It wasn't a good idea to get too close to Kent. Whenever she did she found she wanted to plaster herself against the hot lines of his body.

Could you imagine the look on his face if she did? If she'd had a sense of humour left she'd have laughed.

He continued to stare at her and she shrugged. 'I haven't seen you around for a few days. It suddenly occurred to me that you might've caught whatever I had.'

'Nope.'

'That's good.' She edged closer to the phone, but wondered what he'd do if he did get sick. How long would it be before someone found him? She wanted to ask if he had a plan in case that happened, but she knew if she did he really would tell her to go to blazes. So she didn't. She picked up the phone instead.

Then dropped the receiver back in the cradle. She'd so busily analysed the note for a clue to Kent she hadn't given a moment's thought to what it might mean.

More proof of an addled brain.

'Something wrong?'

'No.' She bit her lip and stared at the note. 'I just don't know why Jacob would call me.' Unless there was an emergency.

'Who is he?'

'A neighbour.' She shook her head. 'Actually he's my neighbour's son. The neighbour that fell ill, you remember?'

'I remember. You had to call her.' His lips lost some of their tightness. 'Once I got you out of the clothes-line.'

'He works in Brisbane now. Oh, I hope his mum is OK. I hope nothing has happened at Geraldine's Gardens. I hope…'

If there was an emergency Marty or Frank would ring her, surely. Unless the emergency was about Marty or Frank!

With a muttered oath, Kent strode over. 'There's only one way to find out.' He took the note and punched in the number scrawled along its base. 'Ask him.' He pushed the receiver into her hand.

His curt tone had the desired effect and, before she could go off into another disaster scenario, Jacob had picked up the phone at the other end of the line. 'Hello?'

'Jacob, it's Josie Peterson. I got your message.' She abandoned pleasantries. 'Please tell me everyone is OK.'

'Sure they are. I didn't mean to worry you, Josie.'

She clutched her chest and sent Kent a smile. He shook his head, but his lips twitched. 'That's good news. Is your mum recovering?'

'Yes, she is. Look, Josie, I didn't know if I should call you or not, it's just…'

'Yes?'

'Marty and Frank have had a team of surveyors in at Geraldine's Gardens.'

She blinked. They had? She searched her mind for a plausible reason. Maybe there was some kind of mine subsidence in the area or… Her mind went blank.

'They've also had in a fancy property developer from the city.'

Her jaw dropped. She could feel Kent angle in on that straight away, so she hauled it back up. 'Uh-huh.' She couldn't manage much more for the moment.

'I don't know what they're up to, but I don't like it. I think you should come home and find out what's going on.'

So did she. 'I'll leave this afternoon.'

'Good.'

'Thanks for letting me know, Jacob.'

'It's the least I could do after everything you've done for Mum. If there's anything else we can do…'

'Thank you, but I'm sure it's nothing to worry about.'

Marty and Frank were her brothers. There'd be a perfectly logical explanation.

But then again…

You can't trust them. Kent's accusation pounded through her.

'Problem?'

After what he'd said about her and her brothers she had no intention of confiding in him. Not that he'd want her to, of course. 'Nothing I can't handle.' She pressed her hands tightly together. 'Though I'm afraid I have to cut my holiday short.'

'I heard.'

She swallowed. 'I guess it's only by three days.'

She wanted him to say something, anything. He shrugged and turned away. With a heart that flapped like a floundering fish, Josie stepped around him and left.

She was ready to leave in under two hours. That was, her bags were packed and she'd driven into Martin's Gully to say goodbye to Clancy and Liz. And Bridget. Bridget had been busy on tennis-club business but Liz had promised to pass on Josie's goodbyes.

They'd made her promise to ring and tell them she'd arrived home safely. They'd made her promise to return for a visit. Her heart ached, but she'd smiled brightly and promised on both counts.

Now all that was left was to take her bags out to the car, hand the cabin key back to Kent and hug Molly goodbye.

She didn't want to do any of those things. She wanted

to unfold the sofa bed and dive beneath its covers. She
didn't. If Jacob had spotted surveyors and property devel-
opers at Geraldine's Gardens then so had the rest of
Buchanan's Point. And those who hadn't would've been
filled in by those who had. Speculation would be rife. Not
that she could blame them for that. Her own mind seethed
with it too.

What on earth were Marty and Frank up to?

A property developer? She gulped. The townsfolk of
Buchanan's Point wouldn't want their seaside village
turned into the latest tourist destination, with all its asso-
ciated high-rises and traffic. They were happy just to meet
the passing trade from the nearby hotspots.

At least the deeds to Geraldine's Gardens were in her
name, so Marty and Frank couldn't sell it out from under
her. And they couldn't force her to sign anything against
her will either.

Molly whined and pressed against her legs. Josie
dropped to her knees and buried her face in Molly's fur.
'At least you'll miss me,' she whispered. From the moment
Josie had hauled out her suitcases, Molly had done her
level best to get underfoot. Josie was grateful to her for it.

But she couldn't delay any longer. Not if she wanted to
be home before dark.

Who cared about the dark?

Heaving a sigh, she pushed herself upright and shuffled
over to her bags. She heaved them up then, dragging her
feet, teetered to the door and dumped them outside. Kent
jumped up from his seat at the end of the veranda.

How long had he been there? Josie gulped and gasped and
coughed and found it near impossible to breathe. 'I, umm…'

He kind of half scowled, his nose curling up at one

corner. He scuffed the toe of a work boot in a patch of dirt. 'Thought you might need a hand with your bags.'

Great. Was he escorting her off the premises? She bet he had his cleaning equipment out before her car reached the end of the driveway. She bet he couldn't wait to erase all evidence of her stay here. After her rant at him on Monday, she didn't much blame him. If she hadn't attacked him like some shrill fishwife then this goodbye scene might be a whole lot—

She slammed a halt to that thought.

Still, it didn't seem right for things to end like this.

'Thank you. I'd appreciate that.' She didn't smile. She couldn't. Not that it mattered. Kent didn't so much as glance at her as he seized both bags and strode off towards her car. Trademark Kent—no backward glances.

His lean denim-encased legs ate up the distance. She wished she could freeze-frame time and drink in her fill. Not just of him, but of Eagle Reach too. She wanted to feast her eyes on Eagle Reach, and Molly, but mostly on him. She wanted to feast her eyes on him, unimpeded, and fix him in her mind forever.

He's already there.

She spun away and stumbled back into the cabin, tripping over Molly in the process. 'Sorry, girl.' She patted Molly's head, drawing comfort from her warmth. She scanned the single room one final time. Her eyes stung. Resolutely ignoring them, she swung her handbag over her shoulder, shoved the key to the cabin in her pocket and picked up her box of groceries.

'C'mon, Molly.' She tried to do a Kent—no backward glances—but she couldn't quite manage it. She glanced longingly around the room once more before she shut the door behind her.

Kent's shadow fell across her as she turned away from the cabin. She stopped and stared at his chest and wished his physical body would follow, wrap around her completely. For one heart-stopping moment she thought it would, but he'd only moved in to take the box from her arms.

Swallowing, she headed for her car. He kept easy pace beside her. The scent of wood and smoke and man swirled around her. She wanted it to last forever.

It lasted until they reached her hatchback.

She didn't even try to avert her gaze when he bent down and placed the box on the back seat. He straightened and Molly started to bark and whine, circling around Josie's legs, pressing against them. It jolted her out of herself. Dropping to her knees, she hugged her, hard. Then drew back to scratch her ears. 'I'm going to miss you.' Molly licked her and tried to climb into her lap. Josie shot to her feet before she disgraced herself and began to cry.

Kent's eyes had darkened to that peculiar shade of navy. She could've groaned at the way it contrasted against the chambray of his shirt. She fished out the key from the pocket of her jeans and dropped it into his hand. 'Thank you.'

He stared at the key for a moment then his fingers closed round it, forming a fist. 'You're welcome.'

She held her breath and prayed he'd sweep her up in his arms and kiss her until her blood sang. Hot, moist killer-kisses. She wasn't stupid enough to dream of a happy-ever-after. She just wanted a big, smoochy, full-body slam.

Wasn't going to happen. But her breath hitched at the thought all the same.

She jolted back to reality when he handed her a business card, his gaze not quite meeting hers. She glanced down at the line drawing of a quaint cottage on the front of the card overlaid with the name: The Station Café.

'"Drive. Revive. Survive."' He quoted a popular driver safety campaign and stared at a point above her head. 'You'll like this place. They do great cake and coffee. It's about halfway between here and Buchanan's Point. A good place to break your journey.'

She nodded and tried for a light, 'Doctor's orders, huh?' but it didn't quite come off. How glad would he be to see the back of her, huh?

His jaw tightened for a moment. 'Promise you'll stop. It's important not to overdo it.'

She tapped the card against her fingers and ordered herself not to cringe. 'I will. Thanks.'

So, this was it?

She dropped her handbag on the passenger seat and closed the door, wiped suddenly damp palms down the front of her jeans. There was still time for Kent to sweep her up…

He strode around the car and opened the driver's door for her and there was nothing for it but to follow him. Disappointment hit her so hard she felt she was wading through fast-drying concrete. Molly started up a long, mournful whine. Josie ducked into the car then got back out. 'This is horrible,' she blurted, motioning to Molly.

There was still time for a kiss. She'd settle for a solitary kiss with the car door between them. She'd—

'I'll look after her.'

Of course he would. She stared at the rigid set of his jaw and told herself to stop living in Cloud Cuckoo Land. It was just… 'I'm sorry we had a falling-out.' She reached up and kissed his cheek, breathed him in one last time. 'Goodbye, Kent.'

This time when she ducked into the car she didn't back out. He closed the door. She started the ignition. Without glancing at him, she wound down the window. He leaned in, brushed the backs of his fingers across her cheek. 'Have a safe journey, Josie.' Then he stepped away.

Josie gulped down the lump in her throat but another one replaced it. She nodded dumbly. When she set off down the drive, this time she didn't look back.

Kent ignored the kick in his stomach as Josie manoeuvred her car down the gravel drive. His chest gave an even bigger kick but he ignored that too. He did lift a hand, though, when she turned out of his driveway and onto the road, but she didn't wave back.

Or toot her horn.

Nothing.

Not that he deserved anything after the way he'd treated her since that ridiculous blow-up. Her sweet, fruity scent lingered around him. The touch of her lips still on his cheek. Bloody idiot to get up on his high horse like that and not come down until it was too damn late.

Too late for what?

Friends, he wanted to shout to the disbelieving voice in his head. They could've been friends.

What use did he have for friends?

He scowled. She was better off without him. And he was better off without her as a distraction. Tempting him with a life he'd promised never to return to.

He released Molly's collar and she bolted down to the end of the drive, but Josie's car had already disappeared. Molly whined then jumped up and down on the spot as if searching for one last glimpse of Josie. When that didn't work she turned and gazed at him, her head low, and he suddenly understood where the term 'hangdog' came from.

He understood exactly how she felt too. 'C'mon, Molly.' He patted his thigh but she ignored him and slunk off to Josie's cabin. He turned and headed back towards the house, then, with a bitten-off curse, swerved to followed her.

He found her laid across the doorway, head on paws and her big, liquid eyes downcast. 'She misses you too, Moll.'

Molly's tail didn't give even the tiniest of thumps. Kent had an unaccountable urge to lie down beside her.

Don't be such a bloody fool. He had cattle that needed attending to.

He didn't leave, though. He didn't lie down either. He pushed open Josie's door and stared at the room behind it.

The cabin was spotless. Its blankness reproached him. Not a scrap of litter, no accidentally abandoned socks, not even the newspaper. Nothing of Josie remained except the tang of her scent in the air.

Molly barrelled straight into the room and climbed up onto the sofa as if that would somehow connect her to Josie. He didn't have the heart to drag her off again. He sat down in the hard chair and pulled in great lungfuls of the sweet air.

CHAPTER ELEVEN

MARTY and Frank's cars lined the circular drive when Josie finally turned in at the gates to Geraldine's Gardens. Her heart didn't lift at the sight of her home. The evening seemed grey, lacking colour, although light spilled from the house. As if expecting her, Marty and Frank burst out of the front door then came to startled halts.

At the same time.

Climbing out of her car, she felt herself moving through that quick-setting concrete again. Behind her a large van turned in at the drive, its headlights temporarily blinding her as it pulled in behind her hatchback.

Marty and Frank skulked on the veranda, shoulders slightly hunched. Neither came forward, so Josie found herself greeting the man who stepped down from the cabin of the truck. 'May I help you?' Her throat felt strangely dry.

'Ted O'Leary from O'Leary's Removals,' he said cheerfully, sticking out his hand.

Josie shook it. 'I think there's been some mistake.'

He consulted his clipboard. 'This Geraldine's Gardens?'

'It is.' She couldn't believe how normal her voice sounded.

'Then no mistake, miss. We have instructions from a Mr Marty Peterson to have the house cleared by morning.'

'With instructions to take it where?'

He checked his clipboard again. 'Into storage.'

Marty finally jogged down the steps to join them. He smiled brightly, but perspiration gleamed on his upper lip. 'It was going to be a surprise for you, Josie.'

His fake jovial tone had her bile rising. She swallowed it back. 'It's certainly that.' Again the calm, measured tone. 'I think you'd better tell Mr O'Leary you've wasted his time and that his services will not be required today.'

Without another word she turned and walked up the three tessellated-tile steps to the ornate wrap-around veranda and started for the door. Frank stepped in front of her. 'There's no need to take on like this,' he blustered, though she noticed his hands shook. 'You need to at least hear—'

She stepped around him, ignoring the drone of his voice. 'Tomorrow,' she said firmly, cutting across him. 'I'll speak to you both tomorrow.'

Then she closed the door in his startled face.

Molly refused to budge from Josie's cabin. Unless Kent wanted to physically pick her up, Molly was staying put.

He didn't want to physically pick her up. He didn't want to do much of anything.

Molly wouldn't touch her food either. Kent didn't have much of an appetite himself. In the end, neither one of them ate. In the end they both slept in Josie's cabin.

Kent pulled out the sofa bed, grabbed a blanket and he and Molly lay side by side…on Josie's bed. It wasn't even dark yet. He stared at the ceiling and wondered if she'd arrived home yet, if she'd got home safe.

Why hadn't he asked her to ring him?

Molly whined. He scratched her ears. The light behind

the curtains had almost completely faded now, but there was still enough light for him to miss the colour Josie had created in here. And taken away with her when she left.

He wanted bright lengths of material draped at the windows. He wanted rag rugs on the floor. He wanted prints on the walls.

Tomorrow. He'd drive into Martin's Gully tomorrow and buy lengths of bright material at Liz's store. Maybe Liz would've heard from Josie. He'd order rag rugs from Thelma Gower; hopefully she'd have a couple to go. He'd stop by Rachel Stanton's studio and check out her water colours.

Then he'd lunch with Clancy. Josie would definitely have rung Clancy because Clancy would've made her promise to.

Kent scowled at the ceiling. Clancy was a smart man.

Josie opened the door. 'Heavens, that was quick. I'm really sorry to call you out like this, Steve.'

Having made it inside her house, Josie had found she was lucky to do so when she saw the shiny new locks in place. If she'd arrived when Marty and Frank weren't here she'd have been unable to get in.

'Not a problem, Josie.' He set his tools by the front door and sent her a shrewd glance. 'When it's a question of security and a woman at home alone then we locksmiths don't care what time of the day or night it is.'

She grinned. 'You guys take a professional vow in lock-smith school or something? Like the doctors' Hippocratic oath?' She wished she hadn't said that, the doctor bit; it reminded her of Kent.

'You bet.' He glanced up. 'I'm glad you're home, Josie. The town's been worried.'

'I know. Jacob rang me.'

Steve wielded his screwdriver. 'Town took a vote and told him he had to.' He set about removing the lock.

That news didn't surprise her. Buchanan's Point was a close-knit community. Marty and Frank had never been a part of it. They were known as townies.

Steve was the only locksmith in Buchanan's Point. She'd gone to school with him. Had played spin the bottle in primary school. She could trust him. 'Did you change the locks at Marty and Frank's request?'

'Nope.'

Darn it. She wanted to know what excuse they'd given. She knew Steve would've asked for one. Which might be why they hadn't used him for the job.

'They hired a mate of mine from Diamond Head.' He winked. 'We went to locksmith school together. He told them I was closer and would be cheaper. But they insisted he do the job anyway. That made him suspicious, like, so he rang me.'

It made her suspicious too. She crouched down beside him. 'Did he find out why they wanted the locks changed?'

'The elder one, what's his name?'

'Marty.'

'He said he'd lost his spare key and rather than risk someone finding it and using it to break in, he thought he'd get the locks changed.'

She bit her lip again. 'He could be telling the truth.'

'Aye, he could be.'

But she could tell Steve didn't believe Marty's story. She didn't either. She jumped to her feet and started to pace. Kent had warned her about this.

She wondered if she rang him and told him he'd been right, if she apologised, if he'd hang up on her.

* * *

Josie glanced at the clock. One o'clock. She picked up the phone and hit redial.

'Mr Peterson's office.'

'Hi, Rita, it's Josie again.'

'I'm sorry, Josie.' Rita clicked her tongue in sympathy. 'He's still in a meeting with a client.'

'This is the fifth time I've called.' She'd rung on the hour, every hour, since nine o'clock this morning.

'I know. I'm sorry.'

She swallowed back her frustration. It wasn't Rita's fault Marty wouldn't return her calls.

'He swears he'll ring you tonight...or, at the very latest, tomorrow.'

Not satisfactory.

Josie didn't say that, though. She said, 'Thank you,' and rang off.

She drummed her fingers against the arm of her chair then picked up the phone and punched in a second number. 'I'm sorry,' a recorded voice started, 'this phone is temporarily out of range or—'

She hung up in disgust. She suspected Frank had turned his cell-phone off deliberately so she couldn't contact him. She massaged her temples. Perhaps if she'd slept better last night she'd feel more able to cope with this. But every time she'd closed her eyes Kent's image had risen up in front of her. Sleep had proven impossible.

She pleated the hem of her blouse with her fingers and wished Kent had asked her to ring him, as Clancy and Liz had done. A longing to hear his voice gripped her again. She'd lost count of the number of times she'd picked up the phone to call him and tell him she'd arrived safely, to tell him he'd been right about her brothers. At the last moment she'd chicken out. He'd have only given one of those derisive laughs and said, 'So what?'

In all fairness, he probably wouldn't, but she'd bet he'd want to. She didn't want that.

What she wanted was impossible.

Kent stepped back to admire his handiwork. Then swore. The material he'd twined around the curtain rods refused to hang in the same soft folds that Josie had created. He'd tossed a tablecloth across the table, he'd shoved flowers haphazardly in a vase and discovered the haphazard-flowers-in-a-vase-look required more skill than his fingers possessed. He'd scattered scatter cushions, he'd hung water colours, he'd thrown rag rugs across bare floorboards and yet it still wasn't working.

It didn't look cosy and inviting. It looked wrong.

Then he got mad. He shooed Molly off the sofa bed and folded it up with one hard shove. He shooed her right outside and slammed the door behind them. But Molly wouldn't budge further than the veranda. 'What's the point?' he shouted at her. 'She's gone.' And she wasn't coming back.

At least he knew she'd arrived home safely. She'd rung both Liz and Clancy. He scowled. And somewhere between yesterday and today the last trace of her fragrance had vanished. Gone. Just like that. He couldn't believe how much he missed it. That fact only fuelled his anger. He started to stride away then swung back to face his dog. 'And if you don't start eating again by tomorrow I'm taking you to the vet.'

At any mention of the vet, Molly usually bolted straight

under the house. This time her ears didn't so much as twitch. With a snort of disgust, Kent strode off.

That evening, however, he carried Molly up to the house and tried to coax her to eat. She lapped at her water, a half-hearted effort, but she still refused to touch her food. At bedtime he carried her into his bedroom and laid her on her usual blanket. At least, it had been her usual blanket before Josie came to Eagle Reach.

Molly spent the night scratching at his door and howling. He wanted to join her. At midnight he relented and let her out. He wondered if a dog could die of a broken heart? Then he called himself an idiot.

By Saturday lunchtime he finally realised Molly was no longer his dog but Josie's. Josie and Molly had connected from the very first moment.

Almost the very first moment, he amended, grinning when he remembered Josie perched in his clothes-line.

With a strange sense of relief he packed an overnight case, made a quick call to Smiley McDonald then bundled Molly into his car and drove into Martin's Gully.

He leapt out at Liz's store. Clancy and Liz stood side by side at the cash register in close conference. Kent didn't waste any time. 'I'm heading for Josie's. Just wanted to let you two know.'

'Good.' Clancy pointed to a case on the floor. 'You can give me a lift.'

'Me too.' Liz hoisted her bag onto her shoulder.

He stared at them and his stomach clenched up so tight he found it hard to breathe. 'Why?' he barked. Had something happened? 'Is she OK?' He wanted to punch something.

'She's fine.' Liz walked around the counter and took his arm. 'We'll explain on the way.'

He didn't say anything more, just grabbed their cases and shot them in the back of his four-wheel-drive, his face grim as he waited for them to climb into the car.

Josie removed Mrs Pengilly's cup and saucer from the arm of her chair as the elderly woman's head began to nod. The doorbell sounded, twice in quick succession. She darted a glance at her guest then padded down the hallway in her bare feet. 'Shh.' She opened the door, finger to lips, then drew back and folded her arms.

Marty pointed a shaking finger at her, his face red. 'You…you had the locks changed.'

'Yes, I did. As neither of you,' she took in Frank with her glance, 'left me a spare key or would answer my calls yesterday, I had no choice.'

'No choice? Nonsense,' Frank snapped, pushing past her.

'I had errands to run. I can't leave a place like Geraldine's Gardens unlocked and unattended.'

'But…but…' Marty followed her down the hall.

'Yes?' She lifted an eyebrow, careful to keep a pleasant smile on her face.

He eyed her warily then pasted on a smile and pulled her to a stop, fake jovial again. 'We have great news.'

She couldn't help feeling he was getting cues over her shoulder from Frank.

She turned. Frank sent her a huge smile too.

'Good news?' she asked. They both nodded eagerly. 'Good.' She rubbed her hands together. 'I love good news. You'd best come into the formal lounge.' It was the room they preferred anyway. 'Mrs Pengilly is dozing in the family room.'

Marty's smile fled. 'What's she doing here?'

'She's my friend. That's what she's doing here.' She closed the door to the formal lounge and prayed Mrs Pengilly was a sound sleeper. 'Do you have a problem with that?'

'No, no.' He backed down and made straight for her father's chair.

'Damn Nosy Parker, though,' Frank muttered, throwing himself into the one opposite. The one she normally used.

She perched on the edge of the sofa. 'It's what I love about this place. Everyone looks out for everyone else.'

Marty and Frank exchanged glances and Josie's heart sank. She just knew she wasn't going to like their good news.

They wanted her to sell her house.

Oh, that news didn't surprise her. They'd been telling her for years that the place was too big for her, too much to keep up with. Part of her agreed, but it didn't mean...

Given time she'd fill it with people. Somehow.

But they had a buyer already lined up, a property developer. And they had a contract ready for her to sign.

Marty pushed his solid silver and gold plated pen, the one he normally guarded with his life, into her hand and pointed. 'Sign there and there.'

'But I want to think about it first.'

Both men started talking at her at once, gesturing wildly, pacing up and down in front of her. Panic spiked through her. Her shoulders edged up towards her ears as walls started to close in around her.

'This is a once-in-a-lifetime chance, Josie.' Marty slapped a hand to the contract. 'You'll never be offered such a good price again.'

He was probably right. The amount offered was obscene.

'And you won't have to work again either if you don't want to,' Frank added. 'And you'll be helping the town.'

'Exactly.' Marty thumped another hand to the contract. 'At the moment it's dying a slow death.'

Her head shot up at that. 'Nonsense.'

'This will make sure it doesn't,' Frank rushed in with a warning glare at Marty.

She bit her lip. He might have a point. They weren't proposing to knock down Geraldine's Gardens and build a high-rise in its place. They were talking about a very exclusive, understated resort. Very swish, with the house and grounds of Geraldine's Gardens incorporated into the overall design. They'd shown her the projected plans. She couldn't deny the tastefulness of the enterprise. But...

'It'll be good for you, it'll be good for the community and it'll be good for us.'

'Good for you how?'

'For a start, we'll have peace of mind knowing you're taken care of. You deserve that after the way you looked after Dad.'

Frank's words hit the sore, needy part of her heart right at its very centre.

Marty patted her hand. 'You're our little sister. We want to see you settled.'

She gulped. She just needed to sign the contract and then...'What was the moving van about?'

'The buyer wants to start work immediately. We wanted to clear the way for things to move as quickly as they could once you got back and signed the contract.' Marty spread out his hands. He still clutched the contract in one of them.

'We didn't think you'd have any objections. We're just looking out for you, Jose.'

The only person in the world to call her Jose had been her father. She leapt up and thrust Marty's pen at him. 'Mrs Pengilly is due for her medication.'

And she fled. She leaned against the wall outside the door of the room, fingers steepled over her nose as she drew in several breaths. All she had to do was sign then she, Marty and Frank would all be one big, happy family.

Somehow the picture didn't quite fit.

When had they arranged all this? Before her holiday?

For the hundredth time that day she wished Kent were here. Not for any other reason than to rest her eyes on him, to breathe in his wood-smoke scent.

Mrs Pengilly's medication. She roused herself, pasted on a bright smile and breezed into the family room to find Mrs Pengilly's chair empty. The doorbell rang.

'Hope you don't mind,' Mrs Pengilly called out when Josie appeared at the end of the hallway, 'but I called for reinforcements.'

Mrs Pengilly opened the door and Josie's jaw dropped as she watched a substantial cross-section of the townsfolk of Buchanan's Point file past her and into the formal lounge. She followed in their wake, dazed.

'What the…? This is a private matter,' Marty shouted. 'What do you think you're doing?'

Jacob sent Josie an encouraging smile. 'We just want to make sure Josie has all the facts she needs to make an informed decision, that's all.'

'And it is our town,' Mr Piper called from the back of the group. 'Josie's decision will affect all of us.'

'Josie!' Marty hollered. 'You have to get rid—'

'They're my friends, Marty. I want them here.' She didn't wait for a reply but turned to the assembled crowd. 'Are you all aware of the proposal?'

Jacob nodded. 'Yes.'

It didn't surprise her. Someone's cousin's uncle would be on a board somewhere. 'It's not a high-rise,' she said anyway, just so they knew, 'but a very tasteful and exclusive resort.'

Jacob kind of shrugged. He didn't look very comfortable thrust into the role of town spokesperson. 'Town opinion is split. That's not the point.'

'Ooh, you should hear Josie's idea for a b & b,' Mrs Pengilly gushed. 'It's fabulous.'

'B & b?' Frank rounded on her.

'It was just an idea and—'

'We're getting off the track,' Jacob inserted quickly. 'What you decide to do with Geraldine's Gardens is up to you, Josie. It belongs to you. What we want is for you to know *all* the facts.'

That was the second time he'd said that. 'What facts?'

'That Marty's firm is guaranteed this buyer's business if the deal goes through. And Frank's firm will get the building contract.'

'That's not a secret.' Frank rounded on them. 'We were just telling Josie about all the advantages if the project goes ahead.'

Ha! She should've known. But she couldn't help wondering if Frank had meant to be as honest with her as he now claimed.

Marty swung to her. 'It guarantees Frank and I make partnerships with our firms.'

Weariness descended over her. For some reason she had

never been able to fathom, Marty and Frank had always felt they'd lost out to her financially. They'd both worked hard to achieve partnerships. She couldn't deny that. Did she really have the heart to stand in their way now? If she signed the contract, would they finally feel she'd squared things up?

'Josie?' Jacob prompted.

'I…' She didn't know what to say.

'What do you want?' he persisted.

She didn't get a chance to answer. At that moment an excited dog burst through the door and knocked her off her feet.

'Molly!' She hugged the squirming bundle of fur. She glanced up and her weariness fled. 'Kent!'

'Sorry, she got away from me.' He stopped dead when he saw the crowd assembled in the room. Clancy and Liz peeped around from behind Kent's back and waved to her. Josie hugged Molly and grinned like an idiot.

'Who the hell is this?' Marty shouted in sudden frustration and Josie came back to herself, even though she couldn't seem to quite catch her breath.

She jumped up. 'Everyone, these are my friends from Martin's Gully. Kent, Clancy and Liz. Umm,' she waved her arm at the assembled crowd, 'this is everyone.'

Her mind whirled. Murmurs of greeting sounded around her, but she couldn't make sense of anything. One thing suddenly became crystal-clear. 'Marty and Frank,' she turned to her brothers, 'I can't make a decision on this tonight.'

Her brothers' jaws dropped. Marty's face went so red she swore he'd burst a blood vessel. 'This is all because I wouldn't come and pick you up from that God-forsaken place, isn't it?' he yelled. 'It's some kind of payback.'

She didn't know how many volts of electricity it took

to snap someone to full attention, but his words ensured he had hers.

Completely.

Her voice, though, was surprisingly calm. 'You knew it was a God-forsaken place?'

'Of course I knew,' he spat. 'What do you think I am? Stupid?'

No, but she was. Anger hit her then in thick red waves. Not only had they set all this up so that she was out of the way while they tried to seal their deal, but in their measly selfishness they hadn't even been able to provide her with a decent holiday.

'So you played me for a sucker?' Neither brother said anything. 'And you prettied it all up by feigning concern for me?'

Marty stared at the floor, Frank at the ceiling.

'Oh, and I fell for it, hook, line and sinker, didn't I? What an idiot you must think I am.'

She waited for them to protest, to tell her they really had appreciated the way she'd taken care of their father, that they really did love her.

Nothing.

'Out.' She picked up the contract and slapped it to Marty's chest. 'You too,' she shouted at Frank. 'Take your contracts and your measly, selfish minds and get out. I don't want to see either of you again.'

Marty blanched. 'You can't mean that.'

'But you're our sister,' Frank started, visibly shaken.

Marty took a step towards her, but to Josie's astonishment Molly bustled up between them, hackles raised. Then she drew back her lips to display every single one of her teeth as she growled. Josie pointed to the door. 'Go.'

* * *

Kent stared at Josie and couldn't remember being prouder of anyone than he was of her at that moment. He wanted to grab her up in his arms and swing her around. He wanted to kiss her. He wanted to drag her off to the bedroom and—

He wanted to stay!

The realisation slugged him straight in the gut. But it didn't knock him off his feet. Instead it surged through him and lent him a strange kind of strength. He wanted to stay and it had nothing to do with Molly, or Clancy and Liz, or sticking up for Josie against her brothers.

It had everything to do with him…and her. It was why he'd come, even if he had tried to hide behind all those other reasons.

He shoved his hands in his pockets and studied her as surreptitiously as was possible with a roomful of people studying him too. The sandalwood highlights of her hair gleamed beneath the overhead lights. Her lips, lush and inviting, hinted at exotic delights. Her eyes still blazed from her sudden flash of temper. He'd never seen anything more desirable in his life.

But what if she didn't want him here? His hands curled into fists. What if she didn't want him?

Then he'd become the kind of man she bloody well did want, that was what.

Josie shook herself, tried to unscramble her mind. She turned to Kent, Clancy and Liz. 'What are you all doing here?' She couldn't believe how good it was to see them.

She tried not to feast her eyes too obviously on Kent. Liz and Clancy both burst forward to hug her. She hugged them back. Kent stayed where he was—hands in pockets, glaring moodily at the floor—and her heart burned.

'We were worried what those no-good brothers of yours were up to, lass.'

Liz's eyes twinkled. 'But it appears you didn't need the cavalry after all.'

'No.' Josie gave a shaky laugh. Her audacity in telling her brothers exactly what she thought and sticking up for herself still shocked her. She glanced at Kent. Had he come riding to her rescue too?

He shuffled his feet, rolled his shoulders. 'Since you left, Molly has refused to eat. She's going to have to live with you.'

Her jaw dropped.

He scowled. 'She misses you.'

She hauled it back up. What wouldn't she give to hear him say those self-same words to her?

'We all miss you,' Liz said. 'And I was thinking, if you start up this b & b of yours you're going to need a hand. Since Ted died I've been looking for a change, and I'm a very good cook, you know.'

Clancy shuffled in closer. 'And I know I'm getting on in years, but I'm still handy in the garden.'

Liz folded her arms. 'You'll need a cook.'

Clancy set his jaw. 'You'll need a gardener.'

A huge lump blocked her throat. She glanced at Kent. He stared at Liz and Clancy as if they'd just lost their minds.

His scowl redirected itself to her. 'And you'll need a husband!'

His words knocked the lump clean out of her throat. All conversation in the room stopped.

'What?' She gaped at him.

His scowl deepened as he glanced around the now silent room, at all the avid, curious faces. He rolled his shoulders again. 'Need probably isn't the right word,' he muttered.

'You don't *need* a husband. You probably don't *need* anyone, but I...'

He glanced around the room again and bit back an oath. Grabbing her hand, he dragged her out of the room, out of the front door and around the side of the house. Then he let her go and continued to glare at her.

Josie shook her head. She couldn't have heard him right. He couldn't have said husband. It wasn't possible.

'Doctor,' she babbled. 'I need a doctor.'

'OK, I'll be that too.'

She wanted to throw herself into his arms. So she massaged her temples instead. 'Did you say I needed a husband?'

'Yes.'

'Is this all about me needing someone to look after me and stuff?'

'I took back the word need.'

Another surge of temper and hope shot through her. 'Did you have someone particular in mind?' She wanted to scratch his eyes out. She—

Then he did something she could never have imagined—he dropped to his knees, wrapped his arms around her waist and buried his face in her stomach with a groan. 'I love you, Josie. Me and Molly, we don't function without you.' His arms tightened. 'I miss your laugh. I miss your smell. I miss you.'

He lifted his head and stared deep into her eyes. 'I didn't see at first that there's more strength in your way. There's more strength in a community, in helping people, in building bridges. I want to build that community with you.'

She brushed the hair off his forehead in wonder, traced

the strong planes of his face with her fingertips. This wonderful man loved her? Her vision blurred. 'You love me? Really?'

Everything inside her sang at his nod. 'And you can't function without me?'

He shook his head. 'No.'

Ooh, she knew how that felt. 'I'll let you in on a little secret: I can't function without you either.'

Kent surged to his feet with a whoop and swung her around. She wrapped her arms around his neck and laughed for the sheer joy of it. When he set her back on her feet she reached up and touched his face. 'I love you, Kent Black. I can't imagine anything more perfect than being your wife.'

He dropped a kiss to the corner of her mouth. 'Say that again.'

Heat started to pump through her. She wanted to melt into him and forget the rest of the world. 'I, umm...'

Her breath caught as he trailed a path of kisses down her throat. He lazily trailed the kisses back up again to nuzzle her ear. 'You taste divine, Josie Peterson.'

If he didn't kiss her properly soon she'd die.

She drew back to catch her breath. 'I love you.' He'd doubted it. She could see it in his face. 'I love you,' she repeated. She'd never tire of saying it.

His hands came up to cradle her face. 'I thought I'd destroyed any chance I had with you. I thought I'd chased you so far away that... And by the time I realised I loved you so much I couldn't live without you I—'

She reached up and pressed her fingers against his lips, stemming the flood of words, needing to drive the demons from his eyes. 'I love you, Kent. Forever.'

'Forever.' He breathed the word against her fingers.

She nodded then removed her hand and as his lips descended she lifted hers and met him in a kiss that sealed their promise.

MILLS & BOON

Pure reading pleasure

FEBRUARY 2008 HARDBACK TITLES

ROMANCE

The Italian Billionaire's Pregnant Bride *Lynne Graham*	978 0 263 20238 0
The Guardian's Forbidden Mistress *Miranda Lee*	978 0 263 20239 7
Secret Baby, Convenient Wife *Kim Lawrence*	978 0 263 20240 3
Caretti's Forced Bride *Jennie Lucas*	978 0 263 20241 0
The Salvatore Marriage Deal *Natalie Rivers*	978 0 263 20242 7
The British Billionaire Affair *Susanne James*	978 0 263 20243 4
One-Night Love-Child *Anne McAllister*	978 0 263 20244 1
Virgin: Wedded at the Italian's Convenience *Diana Hamilton*	978 0 263 20245 8
The Bride's Baby *Liz Fielding*	978 0 263 20246 5
Expecting a Miracle *Jackie Braun*	978 0 263 20247 2
Wedding Bells at Wandering Creek *Patricia Thayer*	978 0 263 20248 9
The Loner's Guarded Heart *Michelle Douglas*	978 0 263 20249 6
Sweetheart Lost and Found *Shirley Jump*	978 0 263 20250 2
The Single Dad's Patchwork Family *Claire Baxter*	978 0 263 20251 9
His Island Bride *Marion Lennox*	978 0 263 20252 6
Desert Prince, Expectant Mother *Olivia Gates*	978 0 263 20253 3

HISTORICAL

Lady Gwendolen Investigates *Anne Ashley*	978 0 263 20189 5
The Unknown Heir *Anne Herries*	978 0 263 20190 1
Forbidden Lord *Helen Dickson*	978 0 263 20191 8

MEDICAL™

The Doctor's Royal Love-Child *Kate Hardy*	978 0 263 19867 6
A Consultant Beyond Compare *Joanna Neil*	978 0 263 19871 3
The Surgeon Boss's Bride *Melanie Milburne*	978 0 263 19875 1
A Wife Worth Waiting For *Maggie Kingsley*	978 0 263 19879 9

0108 Gen Std LP

Pure reading pleasure

FEBRUARY 2008 LARGE PRINT TITLES

ROMANCE

The Greek Tycoon's Virgin Wife *Helen Bianchin*	978 0 263 20018 8
Italian Boss, Housekeeper Bride *Sharon Kendrick*	978 0 263 20019 5
Virgin Bought and Paid For *Robyn Donald*	978 0 263 20020 1
The Italian Billionaire's Secret Love-Child *Cathy Williams*	978 0 263 20021 8
The Mediterranean Rebel's Bride *Lucy Gordon*	978 0 263 20022 5
Found: Her Long-Lost Husband *Jackie Braun*	978 0 263 20023 2
The Duke's Baby *Rebecca Winters*	978 0 263 20024 9
Millionaire to the Rescue *Ally Blake*	978 0 263 20025 6

HISTORICAL

Masquerading Mistress *Sophia James*	978 0 263 20121 5
Married By Christmas *Anne Herries*	978 0 263 20125 3
Taken By the Viking *Michelle Styles*	978 0 263 20129 1

MEDICAL™

The Italian GP's Bride *Kate Hardy*	978 0 263 19932 1
The Consultant's Italian Knight *Maggie Kingsley*	978 0 263 19933 8
Her Man of Honour *Melanie Milburne*	978 0 263 19934 5
One Special Night... *Margaret McDonagh*	978 0 263 19935 2
The Doctor's Pregnancy Secret *Leah Martyn*	978 0 263 19936 9
Bride for a Single Dad *Laura Iding*	978 0 263 19937 6

0208 Gen Std HB

MILLS & BOON®

Pure reading pleasure

MARCH 2008 HARDBACK TITLES

ROMANCE

The Markonos Bride *Michelle Reid*	978 0 263 20254 0
The Italian's Passionate Revenge *Lucy Gordon*	978 0 263 20255 7
The Greek Tycoon's Baby Bargain *Sharon Kendrick*	978 0 263 20256 4
Di Cesare's Pregnant Mistress *Chantelle Shaw*	978 0 263 20257 1
The Billionaire's Virgin Mistress *Sandra Field*	978 0 263 20258 8
At the Sicilian Count's Command *Carole Mortimer*	978 0 263 20259 5
Blackmailed For Her Baby *Elizabeth Power*	978 0 263 20260 1
The Cattle Baron's Virgin Wife *Lindsay Armstrong*	978 0 263 20261 8
His Pregnant Housekeeper *Caroline Anderson*	978 0 263 20262 5
The Italian Playboy's Secret Son *Rebecca Winters*	978 0 263 20263 2
Her Sheikh Boss *Carol Grace*	978 0 263 20264 9
Wanted: White Wedding *Natasha Oakley*	978 0 263 20265 6
The Heir's Convenient Wife *Myrna Mackenzie*	978 0 263 20266 3
Coming Home to the Cattleman *Judy Christenberry*	978 0 263 20267 0
Billionaire Doctor, Ordinary Nurse *Carol Marinelli*	978 0 263 20268 7
The Sheikh Surgeon's Baby *Meredith Webber*	978 0 263 20269 4

HISTORICAL

The Last Rake In London *Nicola Cornick*	978 0 263 20192 5
The Outrageous Lady Felsham *Louise Allen*	978 0 263 20193 2
An Unconventional Miss *Dorothy Elbury*	978 0 263 20194 9

MEDICAL™

Nurse Bride, Bayside Wedding *Gill Sanderson*	978 0 263 19883 6
The Outback Doctor's Surprise Bride *Amy Andrews*	978 0 263 19887 4
A Wedding at Limestone Coast *Lucy Clark*	978 0 263 19888 1
The Doctor's Meant-To-Be Marriage *Janice Lynn*	978 0 263 19889 8

0208 Gen Std LP

Pure reading pleasure

MARCH 2008 LARGE PRINT TITLES

ROMANCE

The Billionaire's Captive Bride *Emma Darcy*	978 0 263 20026 3
Bedded, or Wedded? *Julia James*	978 0 263 20027 0
The Boss's Christmas Baby *Trish Morey*	978 0 263 20028 7
The Greek Tycoon's Unwilling Wife *Kate Walker*	978 0 263 20029 4
Winter Roses *Diana Palmer*	978 0 263 20030 0
The Cowboy's Christmas Proposal *Judy Christenberry*	978 0 263 20031 7
Appointment at the Altar *Jessica Hart*	978 0 263 20032 4
Caring for His Baby *Caroline Anderson*	978 0 263 20033 1

HISTORICAL

Scandalous Lord, Rebellious Miss *Deb Marlowe*	978 0 263 20133 8
The Duke's Gamble *Miranda Jarrett*	978 0 263 20137 6
The Damsel's Defiance *Meriel Fuller*	978 0 263 20141 3

MEDICAL™

The Single Dad's Marriage Wish *Carol Marinelli*	978 0 263 19938 3
The Playboy Doctor's Proposal *Alison Roberts*	978 0 263 19939 0
The Consultant's Surprise Child *Joanna Neil*	978 0 263 19940 6
Dr Ferrero's Baby Secret *Jennifer Taylor*	978 0 263 19941 3
Their Very Special Child *Dianne Drake*	978 0 263 19942 0
The Surgeon's Runaway Bride *Olivia Gates*	978 0 263 19943 7